VOLUME TWO

BOOK ONE

*THE SACRED BLOOD*

BY

DWAYNE ANTHONY MADRY

Printed in the United States of America

First Printing, 2024

Cover Design by JessHavok

ISBN 978-1-963089-27-1

www.SAHAEL.com

# Intoduction into Sahael

In a world shrouded in oppression and turmoil, four young princesses unearth their innate power to restore their homeland's faded splendor. Confronted by daunting societal constraints and the looming specter of ethnic annihilation, they set forth on an odyssey of self-discovery and empowerment, challenging the shackles of tyranny.

Amidst this tumultuous backdrop, Oadira, a princess of extraordinary prowess, wields her mystical gifts to outmaneuver her adversaries, ascending as the formidable Black Madonna–a beacon of upheaval and metamorphosis. Guided by the ancient flame, Oadira embarks on a perilous quest to reclaim Sahael and forge a brighter tomorrow for her people, braving a gauntlet of new trials and tribulations.

Meanwhile, the tale unfolds upon Princess Aamira of the illustrious Yoruban lineage, initially reluctant to forsake her life of opulence and ease. Yet, as the harsh truths of reality unfurl before her, she stands at a pivotal crossroad–compelled to embrace her fated legacy and ancestral ties or forsake them, jeopardizing the chance to rescue her imperiled kin.

CHAPTER CONTENTS

# PART ONE

# KHARTOUM PALACE

# NATAS' INVASION OF SAHAEL

# PROLOGUE: NATAS' INVASION OF SAHAEL

THE TRI-CITIES OF SAHAEL

Aarde, June 19th, The Age of Enlightenment

"The Sahaelian gates are going to be destroyed!" King Regent Enqi yelled as he stepped from the portal created by Njiru's Emerald ring on his left middle finger. Sweat dripped from Enqi's wide nose and down his muscular bare chest to a wrap-around skirt. He stood seven feet tall, wearing a Tutankhamun collar and a headdress that matched his turquoise eyes, accenting his dark brown skin. A golden Ankh necklace hung from his neck. Even in his kingly regalia, at that moment, Enqi felt as small as a child.

"It can't be true!" shouted Great King Enil as he stood from his throne beside his wife, Great Queen Ninti.

"It is," Enqi confirmed.

He looked at the two empty thrones on the far left, one where he sat next to his wife, Queen Regent Arishkegal, and the empty seat next to King Sekhmet where Queen Morrigan would normally sit. The throne room was familiar to him, as he had sat beside the other three kings for decades now. The tall ceilings were ornate with tiled mosaics; towering columns carved with images of Sahael's greatness and glory. Bright flames lit the area from hanging basins filled with sweet smelling oil. There could be no more regal locale in all of Aarde.

And yet now, the shadows seemed to grow, threatening even this palace with ruin.

"Lord Commander Natas' invading forces have breached the Middle Passage," Enqi continued. "The Orishan Armada has taken out one-fourth of Lord Commander Natas' forces, but it doesn't seem to be enough. Nothing seems to be enough."

Enqi's three fellow kings, Great King Enil, High King Ninqi, and King Sekhmet all stood beside their queenly wives, save Sekhmet, whose wife was mysteriously absent. Each was dressed similar to Enqi, though as an albino, Sekhmet's skin was pale white as opposed to chestnut brown like all the other royals.

Their worried faces evidenced the truth that Sahael was in grave danger.

"Where are our daughters?" High Queen Nergal asked. An anxious expression creased the lines on her forehead. "They've only just received their eyesight. Solomon the Protector of Aarde turned eight balls of Orichalcum into Sapphire, Emerald, Hematite gray, and Turquoise and placed them into the girls' eye sockets. They must be protected."

"They are in the garden chasing fireflies as the sun sets," Sekhmet replied. "They will be fine for now. We need to inform the Sahaelian senate of how deep the invasion has already extended. In a matter of mere hours, Natas has reached the very edge of the crater and the three cities. He is on our doorstep!"

"Why weren't we alerted?" High King Ninqi asked.
"How is all of this possible?" The Queens asked simultaneously.

"This happened right under our noses," Great King Enil said, sitting back down on his throne. "If what you're saying is true, Great King Enqi, Natas has made it from one end of the continent to the other in a single afternoon, before we could even launch a counter offensive."

"Fires are already raging in the forests west of Sahaedron, and south of our current position here in Sahael," Enqi said, wiping sweat from his pale brow. "If the assault continues with its current efficacy, Khartoum Palace will be under siege within 24 hours."

Silence fell in the throne room. Only the crackling of the flames in the hanging platters could be heard.

"We need to find out how much time we have to save as many Alkebulans as we can," King Sekhmet said.

"NeRu's Eye can help us determine where there are holes in the enemy lines," King Enqi said. "I suggest we use it to see beyond sight and determine a path for our people. I will fight and die, if necessary, but I wish for our people to live."

Enqi walked over to the balcony on the south side of the palace, followed by his fellow kings and queens. There sat on a marble pedestal, a large green gem, perfectly round, encased in a gold housing forged in the shape of an eye. The royals gathered around it, opening their minds to the relic.

Instantly, Enqi felt the emotions of his ruling partners. Apprehension wafted in his mind like a thick fog. They were all worried. Sekhmet most of all.

Once the wave of feeling subsided, NeRu's Eye allowed them to see all over the Alkebulan continent, tracking Lord Commander Natas' movements and his invading forces from Narsa. Through NeRu's Eye they spotted invading forces in the Kurukeia Forest on the Middle Passage River. Natas' army was under heavy attack by the Yoruban Navy, who had managed to take out a fourth of his attacking forces.

Even so, Natas continued to push toward Khartoum Palace and the capital city of Sahael.

"The question still remains," King Ninqi said. "How is it that Lord Commander Natas' forces were able to penetrate this far into Alkebulan without us knowing?"

A palace guard rushed in, panting while he leaned on his ceremonial golden spear for support.

"My kings and queens," the guard breathed. "The Senate of Sahael has called an emergency session. Your presence is requested."

The kings and queens rushed out of the palace and into the fading light of early evening, down the front steps toward the Senate building across the plaza. Palace guards bowed as they ran past. Merchants stopped and gazed as their rulers sprinted quickly without any of the pomp and circumstance of normal royal travel. If the common people hadn't realized the unprecedented nature of the moment, they now did.

The senate chambers were filled with over one hundred delegates from across Alkebulan and the four great cities, all sitting on a tiered dais eight rows deep. They wore cream-colored robes with different highlighted accents, evidencing their station and individual bloodlines. Enqi caught glimpses of hushed conversations in seats, with some senators looking scared and desperate.

After a brief traditional horn blow and roll call, the senators turned the time over to the kings and queens. King Sekhmet spoke first, informing the politicians about what the royal couples had seen in NeRu's Eye.

"We must act fast," Sekhmet said, breathlessly. "We can question how Lord Commander Natas made his way across the continent so quickly at a later date. If we don't act now, all of Alkebulan, and the holy land of Sahael, will fall."

"Where is Queen Morrigan?" a female senator asked, looking directly at Sekhmet. She was albino like him. "The kings and queens of Sahael should be united at this moment. King Sekhmet; where is your wife?"

Sekhmet cleared his throat. Enqi knew the man well enough to see his hesitancy. Words needed to be chosen wisely among this body. The politics of this chamber had become heated of late as divisions between the bloodlines became exacerbated. Even in a moment of crisis like this, a perceived slight or impression of weakness could derail any positive progress.

"She is with my daughter, Princess Damisiah," Sekhmet replied. "She was…unable to make it here with us in time, but I assure you, both queen and princess are safe."

The senator seemed satisfied. Enqi knew there had to be more of the story though. He could tell King Sekhmet had told the truth, but there was something hidden there as well. Now was not the time to bring it up though. This chamber would erupt in anger and accusation at the slightest provocation.

An aged senator stood from the second row and held up his gaunt hand. "I say we pass a unanimous resolution giving the Kings and Queens full power and authority to do what was necessary to protect and defend Sahael."

"I second," shouted at least three other senators.

"I will mobilize the Demirrian Aerial Army to impede them from having a straight shot of travel directly to Khartoum Palace," Sekhmet said.

Great King Enil and Great Queen Ninti then addressed the Senate. "We will need permission to remove Sahael's cloud barrier."

The Sahaelian Senate shouted unanimously and agreed to

remove the cloud barriers in Sahael from that day forward.

"We need to come up with a plan quickly," High King Ninqi said, stepping forward. His gray eyes reflected the lights from the torches on the walls. "The Yoruban Navy is getting decimated as Natas' forces advance. We must be precise in how we defend against Lord Commander Natas and his forces. Natas is no ordinary general. He is older than our Educators guessed. I have learned of his knowledge and training. He is cunning, and thus we must be cunning too."

"King Enqi," the albino woman senator said, pointing her finger. "As the administrator of the court and leader of our military forces, what are your plans for our reclamation?"

"We need to warn the people in the Tri-cities of Sahael," Enqi said. "That seems to be Nata's primary target."

"I will warn them," Queen Regent Arishkegal said. She squeezed Enqi's hand tightly. Like her fellow queens, Arishkegal was beautiful with dark braided hair, 6 feet-9-inches tall. Dark skin, pale robes, and gold necklaces made her even more queenly, but her face was a mask of calm. Enqi could feel her worry. He loved her as no man had ever loved a woman.

"Start with Alkebulan City and warn the people," King Enqi said.

"I agree," King Sekhmet said. "Queen Regent Arishkegal, should go and warn the people as soon as possible."

"What of the other provinces?" asked an elderly woman senator holding a gold cane with a ruby at the tip. "My people in Aardian City cannot be forgotten. We are fighters all, and will defend our homeland with our own blood."

"Great Queen Ninti," Enqi said. "Would you travel to Aardian City and warn the people of the impending threat and invasion?"

Great Queen Ninti looked to Great King Enil.

"Go," Enil said, touching his forehead to his wife's. "And warn the people. Help them prepare for Lord Commander Natas' threat."

"High Queen Nergal, please warn the people in Sahael City and help them evacuate as soon as possible," King Enqi said.

High Queen Nergal looked at High King Ninqi who nodded his head in agreement.

"Please be careful and do whatever is necessary to get back to Khartoum Palace," High King Ninqi said.

"Gate Guardians and Navigators, escort Queen Regent Arishkegal, Great Queen Ninti, and High Queen Nergal to each of Sahael's three cities," King Enqi directed.

The guardians standing along the walls of the chamber nodded. The Nubian Guards escorted the queens through the gates and left the presence of the four Kings.

"King Regent Enil, warn the Hausan people and get them to mobilize the Hausan defenses with the Knights, Infantry, and Airmen," King Enqi instructed.

Great King Enil nodded his head and left immediately to Sahaerion accompanied by the Gate Guardians and Navigators.

"Esteemed members of the senate," High King Ninqi bowed. "My fellow kings and I must counsel together in this moment of crisis. With your leave, we would retreat to one of the side chambers to discuss planning and military movements. Once we have a firm plan of action, we will reconvene here later this evening."

High King Ninqi led Enqi and Sekhmet to the left where they closed the doors in a meeting room with a long wooden table and many chairs. A breeze blew in from the open windows, causing the curtains to sway like dancers. He immediately rushed over to a bookshelf and pulled out several rolled maps, laying them out on the table. Enqi watched Nephrophida's Interactive Map as it magically changed from one location to the next depending on where the High King focused his eyes. Ninqi stared at the large clearing to the left of Sahael and rubbed his chin.

"Is that valley where we should meet them in battle?" Sekhmet asked as he studied Nephrophida's Map.

"I will meet Lord Commander Natas' invading forces in the clearing," Ninqi said.

"We have to block the river to prevent the Narsan army from moving any closer to Khartoum Palace," Sekhmet said.

Ninqi nodded and tapped the map with his index finger. "King Sekhmet and I will gather intel on their armies in Sahael City and create a blockade on the Middle Passage Rivers."

"That's a sound strategy," Enqi agreed. "Natas' invading forces will have to get out of their ships and meet you on Sahael's battlefield before they all can enter through the Sahaelian Gates."

Chair legs scraped against the tile floor as High King Ninqi sat down. "We need to understand why Sahael was invaded. What purpose does Natas have? How has he been so successful in so short a time?"

Sweat accumulated on Sekhmet's upper lip. "Lord Commander Natas has taken over Naharis's Realm; he is looking to enact his plan here on Aarde."

"How do you know this?" Enqi asked, eyebrows pinched over his nose.

"Nolongo's prophecy is upon all of Sahael due to my transgressions," Sekhmet said. He leaned over one of the chairs and gazed at the map. "I made the decision to bring Black Albino blood into our lineage by marrying Morrighan. Due to my actions, my people are now cursed and will be enslaved. Thus, saith the prophecy."

"Is Queen Morrighan safe?" High King Ninqi asked.

"Morrighan is safe," Sekhmet said.

"Where is she?" Enqi asked. A twinge of anger bubbled in his stomach. What had Sekhmet done? "Don't think we didn't notice your evasion at Senator Elrik's question."

"She's gone."

"Where?" Ninqi asked, standing once again.

"Lord Commander Natas is invading Sahael looking for something," Sekhmet said, rushing past Ninqi's question. "The whispers of the dead have informed me Lord Natas wants something that's in Sahael."

"Knowing what he wants would be nice to know," King Regent Enqi said. His eyes narrowed as he looked at Sekhmet. "You know what it is, don't you?"

"Lord Commander Natas' sole purpose for invading Sahael is Nzingha's Obsidian key, Njiru's rings, and Nebiriau's bracelets," Sekhmet nodded. "The treasures taken from Nablidah's monument, Nier's monument, Neros's monument, and Nethal's monument that Solomon ordered us to hide years ago in secret."

High King Ninti took a deep breath. "I remember. It was the last thing Natas wanted after we took the Kemite Treasures, preventing the eradication of the ancient, sacred, and divine bloodlines. All he wanted was to prove to Ishtar and Obatala that his plan for the peoples of Aarde was the right plan all along."

"What more do you know more about that plan, Sekhmet?" Enqi asked.

"I don't know that much," King Sekhmet said. "We should probably search the archives for more details."

"But how is it you know why Natas is attacking?" King Ninqi asked, impatience evident in his voice.

"Prior to the ceremony with the princesses where they were given sight, Morrighan and I met with Solomon the Protector of Aarde. It was immediately before he had completed the rituals of placing the Turquoise stones inside of Damisiah's empty eyes," Sekhmet said.

"I remember that day," High King Ninti replied. "Solomon took the two of you aside. You weren't gone for very long."

"It was long enough," Sekhmet said. "Solomon gave us a glimpse across Aarde but bade us to secrecy saying that at some time not very distant, we would need to share it, but not before, so fear would remain in check. I admit, my fear has gotten the better of me, which is why I know he spoke true. From Nablidah's monument and through Morrighan's magic, we observed Damien, son of Natas, infiltrate Naharis's realm disguised as Nethanites. Lord Lieutenant Damien entered Naharis's realm, killing all and everything in their path,"

"You saw this?" Ninti asked, eyes wide.

"Lord Lieutenant Damien had figured out a way to bring his father through Nebuchadnezzar's portal, bypassing Nabopollassar's seal and opening up Nullify's gate for him to pass through with Nineveh's Onyx iris," King Sekhmet explained.

"We must notify King Enil and the queens at once!" Enqi said, slamming his hand against the table.

"What else did you see and hear?" High King Ninqi asked. He held his hand up toward Enqi as if to calm his fellow sovereign.

Sekhmet nodded, feeling sweat trickle down his forehead. "Yes, in our vision a witan man appeared outside the Nelion gates, a witan man from Narsa. After Natas emerged from the other side, his host spirit, a Black natural body in spirit form, took over the

Narsan man's body, making it his own. Lord Commander Natas changed back to his natural skin color of dark chestnut. Afterward, the Narsan man's spirit joined with the other evil souls and united with the Dybbuks to cover his tracks with the help of Vice Uré. Lord Commander Natas then skin-changed back into the Narsan man whose witan skin would allow him the opportunity to create systemic racism through laws to help him put his plan in motion and see it realized."

"Lord Lieutenant Damien has betrayed our trust!" Enqi shouted, voice echoing through the empty meeting room. "He broke the Nairobi laws to see it all happen. He believed in his father's plan all along, despite swearing fidelity and honor to the people of Aarde!"

"Please continue, Sekhmet. Tell us what the both of you saw," High King Ninti said.

"Lord Lieutenant Damien wanted to know how Lord Commander Natas knew Nzingha's Obsidian key was located in Necrosis's burial chamber in Sahael," King Sekhmet continued.

Ninti shook his head. "We don't even know where Necrosis chamber is located. If we did, we might be able to cut off Natas from gaining possession of it. "

"Natas knew Nzinga's Obsidian Key was located in Sahael by killing the Narsan man's soul and then having his spirit join in with the Nabopollassar's obsidian seal. That act revealed it was located in Sahael." Sekhmet said.

A bird cawed outside the window. Other than that, the kings stood silent.

"That is why I'm here now," Sekhmet continued. "This was the time allowed to warn all of you at Solomon's request. He told us that to save Sahael will require the law of sacrifice by all four Sahaelian Kings."

The Law of Sacrifice? Enqi clenched and unclenched his fists. Why had Solomon not told all the kings and queens of this coming catastrophe?

Ninti breathed and leaned over the table; eyes locked on the stone surface. "We all understand what this means."

"We will do whatever is necessary to see Sahael, our bloodlines, and our people safe," Enqi nodded.

King Ninti and King Enqi raised their right hands in the air in the form of a fist, symbolizing that they were ready to fight and defend Sahael and its people.

"I was commanded by Solomon to visit each king and queen personally to retrieve Njiru's rings and Nebiriau's bracelets individually," Sekhmet said.

"We have to keep them out of Lord Commander Natas' hands," High King Ninti said.

Sekhmet nodded. "Once they are in my possession, I will make sure our daughters Oadira, Aamira, Heziara and Damisiah have Njiru's rings placed around their ring fingers and index fingers and Nebiriau's bracelets placed around their wrists. I will visit the Queens and give our bracelets to them individually. We will figure out a way and purpose to unlock Nebiriau's power."

"The queens should be back by morning after spreading the word of the attack." Engi said. "King Ninqi should be back no later than tomorrow afternoon, using the Nairohenge Gates."

"By then, Natas may indeed be at our very doors here at Khartoum Palace," Ninti agreed.

"Then we know what to do," Sekhmet said. "In the meantime, we should fortify the palace forces. The Nubian guards will stay by the sides of the Kings and Queens as is their duty, even if it means death. We should activate all reservists immediately. I will sound the alarm." He held out his hand. "And I need your bracelets now."

Enqi shook his head. "No. As leader of Sahael's armies, it is my duty to meet with the queens about this. You will give me *your* bracelet, and I will pass the word. Besides, I fear there is more to this story you haven't told us."

"Where is Morrighan?" High King Ninqi asked slowly.

Sekhmet's eyes darted toward the ground and then back up to the eyes of the High King.

"You already have Morrighan's rings, don't you?" Enqi asked.

"Yes," Sekhmet admitted. Speaking the words made his cheek twitch.

"Where is Morrighan?" High King Ninqi asked again.

Tears came to Sekhmet's eyes. "Solomon warned us of the fear the images we saw would bring, which is why we couldn't share them. He said…even the bravest of us…would be haunted by them. And he was right."

Enqi stepped forward, dreadlocks swinging over his shoulder. "What did you do?"

Sekhmet looked into the eyes of his friend and colleague. "I sent her away in secret this morning as soon as word reached us of Narsan ships off the coast. Morrighan wanted to take Damisiah to Nablidah's monument in Naharis's Realm located in the deep south in western Aarde where she would be safe. I couldn't let my wife die along with the rest of us. Since Naharis's Realm has already been attacked, we felt it would be safest. I'm not sure if they can make it, but they were to use the Nabtahenge Gates."

Ninti stepped forward and stared at Enqi, face hard as stone. "So, our queens will die too?"

Nodding, Sekhmet sobbed quietly.

"And our daughters?" Enqi asked. All anger had left his body, replaced by fear. "Has your albino blood betrayed them as well?"

"The princesses will survive," Sekhmet breathed. "Though they will pass through many trials before setting foot on Sahael once more. According to Solomon, the gods have laid out a path for them, but there is no guarantee they will walk it. Solomon has faith all will be redeemed, but he can't promise anything. All I know is I couldn't let my wife and daughter die."

"But our wives and daughters?" Ninqi asked, words sharp.

Another sob pulled at Sekhmet's shoulders, and he slumped forward slightly. "I was the bravest, Solomon had said. I was the one least likely to give into fear and yet…I failed all of you, my High King. I failed."

The sound of weeping filled the chamber. Enqi could see the shame burned in his friend's chest like a hot coal. He was sure Sekhmet had convinced himself that no betrayal was taking place so long as he did what he had promised to Solomon. Even so, Sekhmet's wife Morrigan had a chance at survival, while Arishkegal and the other queens would likely die along with their husbands. Sekhmet had condemned his friend's and their wives to death.

Ninqi's hand touched Sekhmet's shoulder.

"You are the bravest of us, Sekhmet," Ninqi breathed. "You have proven that in battled again and again as we have fought beside you. If Solomon said you were the most likely to overcome fear, I can only imagine what Enqi, Enil, and myself would have done with the knowledge you were give. I have faith in Solomon. I have faith in Ishtar and Obatala, the great gods of Aarde. If a path has been laid for our daughters to redeem Sahael and our people, then I will trust it, even if I won't live to see it."

Enqi nodded, though his anger still burned behind his eyes.

"We have much to do," Ninqi continued. "Call the reservists and get our forces ready. Natas will enter the craterlands within the next 24 hours. If the law of sacrifice is required, then we will sacrifice, but not before we each send ten thousand Narsan soldiers to hell."

The sun rose red the following morning. Smoke billowed on the horizon. Troop reports had streamed in throughout the night. Casualties were mounting on both sides. For every Sahaelian that fell, at least three Narsans were killed. Even so, the enemy pushed forward like cockroaches. No matter how many of Nata's troops perished, a hundred more waited in the wings.

By sunrise, Enqi was exhausted. He had written numerous parchments and communicated telepathically with Nubian generals trained in such artes. Sleep called to him, but once High Queen Nergal, Queen Regent Arishkegal, and Great Queen Ninti had finished warning and helping evacuate the three cities in Sahael, they traveled back through the Nairohenge Gates with the Medjay Guardians and the Navigators. It was time for Enqi to deliver the bad news.

"Why did you and our husbands take Njiru's rings and Nebiriau's bracelets from the four monuments in each of the realms?" High Queen Nergal asked as Enqi explained everything to them in one of the royal counsel rooms overlooking the palace gardens.

"I told you," Enqi continued as a warm breeze blew through the silk curtains. "Solomon, the protector of Aarde, sent us on a secret mission to retrieve them individually from the monuments as part of the agreement of restoring the eyes of our daughters." "What in Horus's name made you all think that was acceptable without telling me, your wife?" Arishkegal asked.

Enqi took his wife's hand. "After we retrieved Njiru's rings and Nebiriau's bracelets, Solomon agreed to come to the capital city if all four realms could reconcile for the good of Sahael, Egyptus, and Horn. It was for the good of all Alkebulan. That is why the Sahaelian Houses of government were created, to ensure all four bloodlines were in unison with one another."

"There has to be a reason why Lord Commander Natas wants Njiru's rings and Nebiriau's bracelets," High Queen Nergal said.

"They were initially created by the Ancient Kemites who arrived in Aarde," Enqi answered. "The Ancient Kemites used them to help travel throughout Aarde without needing the Nabtahenge Gates. They used creative ways to travel and avoid the sun, which accelerated and removed their immortality from the bloodline. So, Njiru created rings to help open portals to travel anywhere in Aarde by rubbing one of her rings and arriving at any location she wanted. Nebiriau created bracelets that allowed them to be in the sun and could only be seen by those who share the Ancient, Sacred, and Divine blood. Those that were able to detect Nebiriau's bracelet were seen as people the Kemites could trust."

The queens stood quietly as another gust of wind blew through the open balcony to their left.

“Then we can safely assume some of their technology was used by Lord Commander Natas to gain access into Aarde,” High Queen Ninti said.

“He’s probably using it now in his invasion,” Arishkegal nodded.

“I only know what Solomon showed to Sekhmet and Morrighan regarding the attack,” Enqi replied. “As we all know, Nullify created five gates that could harness Ancient Kemetic power, that was combined harnessing the power of Nebuchadnezzar, Nabopollassar, and Nzinga’s Kemite power. Lord Commander Natas used Nullify’s Gate to create a portal that enabled him the ability to enter Sahael from the Outer Realms of Darkness.”

“Finding a way to close Nullify’s gate and preventing others from entering and traveling to unwanted locations needs to be our priority,” Nergal said.

Enqi shook his head. “Nabopollassar created seals that prevented unwanted threats from entering Aarde, or any of the realms, that could threaten Sahael. But to allow entry, Nzingha created seven ancient keys that allowed others access into Aarde to unknown locations to get past the many seals.”

“I’ve studied as you have,” Ninqi said, staring at Enqi in anger. “An agreement was reached with the Ancient Kemite Supreme leaders Kainoa and Kaimana. Ishtar and Obatala asked them all to come to the city of Katunkumene in Andalusia. In return for saving their bloodline, Kainoa and Kaimana stayed. This allowed Katunkumene the ability to travel to and from Aarde using ancient Kemettian technology, which enhanced Sahael with the ability to protect all Black Alkebulans.”

“What must be done to prevent Lord Commander Natas from achieving his plans?” Queen Regent Arishkegal asked.

“That’s something the four of you would have to decide for yourselves when the time is right,” Enqi said. He could feel their frustration and feelings of betrayal. Morrighan should be here with them to sacrifice as well, but she wasn’t. “You all need to stay behind and assume control of Khartoum Palace; the gate guardians, Navigators, and the Nubian guard will ensure you all stay safe. Here are our bracelets. Give them to our daughters when you feel the time is right. They will protect them and hopefully guide them back to Sahael, if they chose that path.”

“Where is Morrighan?” Ninti spat, not hiding her disdain. “I don’t know,” Enqi said, shaking his head. “Sekhmet sent her and Damisiah off yesterday morning at the first sign of the assault. We can’t worry about that now. We have preparations to make and battles to fight. Now go,” Enqi looked at Arishkegal, wanting to embrace and kiss her, “and may the love of your husbands go with you.”

The queens left, taking the bracelets as instructed. Enqi looked over Nephrophida’s Interactive map one final time. Troop movements were being cut off everywhere.

Natas would likely break through the lines and assault the palace itself by day’s end.

He thought about the hatred the queens felt for Sekhmet and understood their animosity. Still, had their roles been reversed, Enqi couldn’t say for sure whether he would have done any differently. Enqi walked to the Nairostone gates from the Sahaelian Senate chambers. The gray stones stood twelve feet tall, topped by six-foot long rectangular pillars laid horizontal. These gates were capable of transporting thousands of people instantly to any number of designated locations throughout Aarde, so long as the gates on the other side were active. Enqi ordered the Khartoum Palace guards to stay to protect the Sahaelian House and its four levels of government. He also ordered his own legion of soldiers to remain at Khartoum to defend the queens and princesses. If battle arrived at the gates of the palace, the queens would have the best chance of survival with his Yoruban soldiers; the strongest and most highly trained warriors in all of Alkebulan.

As the sun aged toward evening, bells began clanging throughout the city. Enqi ran to the upper balcony of Khartoum Palace that looked out on all Sahael. Before he reached the terrace, Enqi smelled ash in the air. Screams echoed from the outskirts and seemed to draw closer with each second.

Natas had arrived.

Fires burned along the south edge of the city. Below the balcony, Sahaelian senators and elected officials ran from the palace, shouting about reaching the river and evacuating before death could overtake them. Narsan guards stood at attention ready to die if necessary to protect the palace and the royal bloodlines.

The time for King Enqi to join the fight in Sahael city was now. He ran back down the staircase to the center of Khartoum Palace where the Nairohenge Gates remained active.

"Send me to the center of Sahael City! Now!" Enqi ordered the Navigators guarding the gateway in their blue and gold ceremonial robes.

"Yes, King Regent Enqi," the lead Navigator bowed.

The portal between two of the stone doorways swirled and changed from purple to blue. Enqi charged forward, feeling the air around him tingle with electricity as he plunged through the mystical gateway.

Instantly, Enqi arrived in the very center of Sahael city where a second circle of Nairostone Gates stood in the evening sun.

Thousands of people evacuated through the Nairohenge and Nairostone gates. They were traveling to different locations throughout Alkebulan in one of the three empires. Whether the other gates would take them far enough away from Natas' wrath was yet to be seen.

Enqi doubted it very much.

He knew few of his people would survive the night. If Sahael fell in the way he feared it would, the entire continent would be poisoned and uninhabitable by morning.

Still, hope remained. Solomon had made sure of that and had given Sekhmet and Morrighan a glimpse. A path to redemption was already laid, and Enqi's own daughter, Aamira, would be a key part in that bright future.

A high-pitched whistle blew from Enqi's lips as he summoned Olami, his white Sahaelian bear, from the Khartoum palace stables. Within moments, the bear's feet thumped loudly on the cobblestone. Olami was twelve feet long, weighing four thousand pounds. He breathed a gust of hot breath from his nostrils as Enqi patted his coarse fur.

*"We go into battle together one more time, old friend,"* Enqi said telepathically to his trusted companion. *"May we save this people, despite my fears that this will be our last night in Aarde. May you survive even if I don't, my friend. May you hunt in the forests of Sahael as a free bear long after my body is moldering in the dirt."*

Olami snorted loudly and roared as if to say, *'We die together.'* Enqi smiled and quickly hopped on Olami's back.

They rode swiftly from the city's center. Enqi looked at the architecture around him, appreciating the beautiful cobblestone streets and large buildings made of glass, stone, and wood. The homes and commerce structures were all shapes and sizes, made with exquisite workmanship from the finest engineers in Sahael and Alkebulan.

It would be a shame to see them burned.

People ran past Enqi and Olami, fleeing toward the gates, as one of their Kings instead rode toward the growing sounds of battle and the heat of raging fires. Smoke choked the air the closer he drew to the commotion. Even so, he would not pause or hesitate. He would give his own life freely to save even a single Sahaelian resident.

Through the fumes, Enqi spotted Narsan soldiers cutting down anyone too slow to outrun their invasion. Old men cried out as blades tore through their flesh. Even children were not spared. There would be no mercy shown from Natas' forces.

Pale emerald swords of emotional energy materialized in Enqi's hands, glowing hot to the touch. They would taste blood this evening. Just as Enqi prepared to ride Olami forward and begin dispatching enemy soldiers with extreme prejudice, he saw High King Ninqi emerge from a small pond to the left of the advancing army, leading a legion of Orishan Axolotl, Knights, Infantry, and airmen. High King Ninqi rode his water dragon, Drake, as his Orishan archers emerged from the water, attacking the advancing forces. Drake was a one hundred- and sixty-four-feet long dragon, with bluish gray scales and sapphire-colored eyes. Drake's claws were made of Onyx Keratin with impenetrable skin. The creature was a force to be reckoned with, and Enqi had seen Ninqi ride him to victory many times.

Natas would curse the day he chose to face the four kings in pitched battle.

On the right Enqi spotted King Sekhmet charging from the city forest riding on Demirrian rhinoceroses, along with a Demirrian legion of his own. King Sekhmet rode on Rhilas, a white, fifteenfoot tall rhino, weighing three thousand pounds. The rhino roared as it crushed a Narsan soldier under its massive foot, while impaling another on his front horn.

There was no sign of Great King Enil though.

The Orishan and Demirrian forces converged, decimating the Narsan soldiers. Within minutes, a thousand Narsans lay dead. Enqi himself had decapitated at least 40 enemy fighters, sustaining only minor cuts in the process. His speed far outmatched these foreign invaders. Each slash of his blade brought death as Olami charged through the enemy lines, slashing soldiers with his massive claws. Enqi avoided strike after strike, while spilling blood onto the stones of his homeland.

The smoke intensified, but the cry of battle quieted as the remaining Narsans retreated toward the city gates once more.

"I want all of your Nubian guards to head to each of the four realms," Enqi shouted to his fellow kings. "And keep the stewards safe inside the four realms. I want the Gate Guardians and Navigators to travel to undisclosed locations until they're found and summoned back to Sahael during the great gathering of the ancient bloodlines."

"Where is your army?" King Ninqi asked, breathing heavily. Blood dripped from a gash on his left arm, but other than that, he looked well.

"My Army is back inside Khartoum palace," Enqi answered. "They are defending High Queen Nergal, Queen Regent Arishkegal, and Great Queen Ninti, along with princesses Oadira, Aamira, and
Heziara."

"I just received word that Natas' forces have made it past us on the south, and will be hitting the main gates any minute," Sekhmet yelled, turquoise energy sword held over his head.

"We need to get to the clearing gates," Enqi cried. "That's where we will meet Lord Commander Natas once the Sahaelian gates are breached."

The two kings mobilized their armies and marched to the clearing along with Enqi. They climbed off their mounts and ascended the steps to the top of the battlements behind the main gate. Green fields and waterways reached the horizon hundreds of feet below.

The Middle Passage River flowed beneath them through an orichalcum gate as hard as any substance on Aarde. It had been forged in cross-sections of metal with four-inch-square openings that allowed the water to pass through, but nothing else as it plunged into the river. Even the tallest of sailing vessels could pass safely through the gate when opened, but when closed, nothing could penetrate the barrier. Walls of pale-yellow stone, fifty feet tall, stretched for miles in both directions from the gate, barring anyone from entering Sahael from the south.

On the other side of the barricade, fishing vessels burned along the shore, and several sailing ships were under attack from Narsan schooners launching harpoons into the hulls and ripping them to shreds. Bodies floated downstream. The water itself, normally clean and pure, had turned slightly pink from the blood of innocent Sahaelians.

Enqi pointed toward an advancing army on the west side of the river. At least five thousand Narsans shouted a bloodthirsty chant of death and revenge in Natas' hateful language. Several large vessels floated the river at unnatural speeds, smashing into Sahaelian ships and obliterating them as if they had been built from straw.

"Lord Commander Natas and his invading forces will have to meet us out in the open on our terms," Enqi shouted. "If the numbers I'm seeing are correct, based off initial reports, fifty percent of his forces are already decimated. We have a chance!"

"Look!" a soldier shouted. "It's the Tryton! Natas is here! Death follows!"

Enqi gazed on the massive ship below with its red sails. On the front of the vessel was mounted a massive metal skull twenty feet tall. This was Lord Commander Natas' personal yacht, the Tryton. It was terrifying and black, made from unknown materials and had been whispered to be cursed with the spirits of murderers and rapists. Enqi had never believed in such myths before, but seeing the ship now with his own eyes, he understood why sailors would spread such claims far and wide.

"The Tryton is about to crash into the gate!" one of the guards yelled.

"The gates will hold!" another soldier assured.

An explosion rocked the battlements and sent stone shaking at their feet. Enqi ran down the steps to see the gate below them. The barrier door bent inward and cracked under the impact of the speeding ship.

The craft seemed to back up for a moment and slam into the gate again, with a force Enqi could not have imagined or described had he not seen it for himself. The second blow sent shockwaves through the ground and breached the orichalcum. The skull head rammed completely through, tearing the gate from its hinges, and sending stone tumbling from the battlements above. Chunks of masonry splashed to the river along with a dozen Sahaelian soldiers caught off guard by the blast. Other ships followed behind the Tryton, sailing straight up the river toward Sahael.

"Natas isn't stopping to take the port," Ninqi cried from the battlements above as the yacht glided past.

The glowing swords in King Sekhmet's hands dissipated on the wind. "With as fast as they're sailing, Natas will make it to Sahael before we can!"

Enqi wouldn't let that happen.

"We defended Sahael less than an hour ago, and we will do it again!" Enqi shouted up to the kings. "High King Ninqi and King Sekhmet, take your armies to Sahael city. Move as fast as you've ever moved in your life."

The kings and armies ran with a speed that Enqi had not thought possible. Sekhmet held tight to Rhilas the rhino, which charged forward far faster than any man could run. Ninqi climbed back onto his water dragon Drake and took to the skies. Enqi followed behind on Olami's back, easily outpacing the infantry. Sweat dripped from Enqi's nose as he pushed the bear as fast as the beast's legs could go. He could hear his heartbeat and the sound of his breath in his ears. He feared for his people.

They arrived in Sahael City as it burned around them. Already Narsan soldiers had massacred hundreds of innocents, whose bodies lay on the stone streets in their gore. Corpses of witans, white-skinned foreigners with fine hair and slender frames, lay on the streets as well, proving that not only had Natas conscripted the Narsans to his invasion, but the surrounding nations as well. Only the primary striking force were Narsan. No wonder Natas had brought so many soldiers to bear; he had half the planet working with him to depose Sahael from its place as the most powerful nation in Aarde.

A great battle was already raging. Among the dead were many of Great King Enil's Hausan soldiers. Enil and his army were in a pitched battle among the buildings and squares of Sahael with Lord Commander Natas and his mixed-race forces.

"Let's help him!" King Sekhmet and High King Ninqi said in unison. Their soldiers cheered.

"No!" Enqi cried. "I need you both to exercise caution and not engage Lord Commander Natas' armies. Great King Ninqi! Move your army through the city without engaging,"

"But the battle!" Ninqi stuttered.

"Trust me! Look!"

The witan soldiers used weapons that would explode in fire and ash when thrown. While the Sahaelian forces were ten times as skilled as the attackers, their strange and destructive orbs wreaked havoc wherever they detonated.

"Don't get too close!" Enqi ordered. "Those balls they're throwing will tear your lines to shreds."

"Look!" yelled Sekhmet, pointing to the sky.

Suddenly Great King Enil appeared above with the Hausan aerial infantry. Enil rode Grave, his large Griffon, whose wingspan was eight feet wide and golden-brown, with powerful onyx talons. Other griffons followed, mounted by soldiers shooting arrows with the precision of the greatest archers ever known. A fog descended, blanketing the Narsan and witan soldiers. They cried out in fear as death descended.

The Aerial Military rained down diamond-tipped arrows on the weapon-wielding Narsans. The arrows came from out of the clouds, piercing Sahael's cloud barrier as the barrage fell upon their heads with absolute precision. The griffins carried large rocks in their talons and dropped them on the invaders as well. Hundreds of invading skulls were crushed on impact. Their lifeless bodies fell to the ground as blood filled the cracks between the cobblestones. Another set of arrows came down sideways, severing arms and legs. Narsans screamed on the ground in agony. This was all done as cloud fog made it impossible for the Narsans to see anything that disadvantaged them.

The Orishan Knights controlled the river and lake on their command ship Axolotl. They attacked the enemy vessels with the ferocity of the water dragons on their bloodline's sigil. Natas' ships sank to the bottom of the river floor.

The Axolotl were now in their natural element. No sailing fleet could match their skill, or the magic abilities afforded them by the water. King Ninqi spoke directly to their minds, allowing them to swarm and attack like a school of ravenous sharks. They took the lives of any Narsan in the water, dragging them deeper into the river as they drowned.

"The advantage is ours!" Shouted Enqi as he and members of the Orishan and Demirrian forces advanced, slaughtering what remained of the invaders, pushing them back toward the river.

But the advantage dematerialized almost instantly. A loud buzzing sound filled the skies and echoed through the burning city. Enqi looked up to see a dozen airships, large, ballooned vessels with spinning propellers, flying in from the south. He had seen small ships like these used in celebration parades since childhood. The propellers would be spun by hand while attached to a string or band of stretchable reed from the river, and then would spin on their own and fly a bit through the air. He never imagined they could be enlarged to this size and used in warfare. Each appeared to be over one hundred feet long with propellers that were definitely not being spun from a length of supple reed. These gigantic aerial warships had the words *Life, Love, Light, and Luck* displayed on their ballooned backs in the language of the Narsans in the form of a square symbol.

Large bombs began to drop, exploding with intense purple fire and smoke. Like with the airships themselves, Enqi recognized the devices, as they had been used in mining operations for many years. Obsidian nitrate bombs. Once again, the Narsans had turned a tool into a weapon, with far more destructive force than anyone thought possible. Buildings crumbled as chunks of stone flew through the air after every explosion, killing even more Sahaelian soldiers.

The buildings shook, masonry crumbled, and Enqi's teeth vibrated every time an explosion ripped through the city. Olami darted to and fro in terrified bursts, unsure what was happening.

*"Peace, my friend!"* Enqi spoke to the bear's mind. *"Steady! Now is not the time for fear!"*

Great King Enil flew high, destroying several small Narsan airships with his sword and the arrows of his forces, but Grave the griffin was hit in the wing by shrapnel from a blast and forced to return Great King Enil to the ground before flying away to rest. "Retreat!" Ninqi ordered. "Retreat!"

After a few minutes, the cloud fog started to dissipate, and the Narsans began parachuting off their airship carriers, going on the offensive. The whole atmosphere was filled with arcane grey metal and blinding rays of light. Arrows shot in all directions, taking out hundreds more of the Hausan aerial infantry, killing their griffon mounts and sending them plunging thousands of feet to their deaths. Soldiers landed all around Enqi with wet slaps of blood and burst organs.

Within moments, Great King Enil's entire aerial Hausan infantry was nearly wiped out. Enil ordered his Hausan cavalry to attack immediately. They charged in kamikaze-fashion with diamond-tipped double spears emerging from the shadows, impaling Narsans through their chests.

Great King Enil ordered his cavalry to kill the wounded Narsans making sure that they would never be able to come back with any chance of hurting the people in Sahael city.

Yet the Narsan and witan forces kept coming.

And coming.

And coming.

Wave after wave descended on Sahael, filling the streets with corpses high enough they would need to climb over them to continue fighting.

Enqi fought and killed as the sun set over the crater's edge in the west. He was in total shock, his palms sweaty. The number of enemies he had killed could no longer be counted. His arms felt heavy with fatigue. The sky grew steadily darker as the last rays of sunlight filtered through the high clouds.

A building exploded to his left, launching him off Olami's back and into the air. Enqi landed hard on several dead bodies, which cushioned his fall and kept him from breaking any bones on the pile of rubble. He rolled quickly and came to his feet, reforming the energetic swords in his hands.

"Olami! Come!" Enqi cried.

But the bear didn't respond.

There, among the smoke and debris, lay Olami. The white bear shifted and groaned. Red blood covered his pale ribs where large shards of stone protruded. Enqi ran forward and threw his arms around his mount, letting his swords dissolve like water between his fingers. He could smell the blood even above the smoke and ash choking the air.

"Olami," he whispered.

Another guttural groan escaped the bear's throat as he stood on shaky legs.

"Olami," he said again in a soothing tone. "You've done well, old friend. The time has come to rest. Run into the forest and heal from your wound. If you smell Arishkegal and my daughter Aamira at any time while you roam the trees, protect them. Your time to die is not yet. Your time to protect is now."

Olami roared, though weak and with obvious pain. The bear nodded and limped through the smoke toward the forest. Enqi felt suddenly alone. He knew that he would never see Olami again. He would likely never see Arishkegal or Aamira again.

Footsteps echoed in the courtyard behind Enqi. He turned to see 40 Narsan and witan soldiers march through the fumes.

A single tear fell from Enqi's eye. He wiped it as a green sword once again formed in each hand. He screamed as he charged the enemy forces, leaping into the air and slicing indiscriminately. Men bellowed and died all around him. A red fury burned behind his eyes as he hacked and slashed, feeling the blood of Narsans splatter his face and arms. Within moments, the entire cadre of soldiers lay dismembered at his feet. Warm gore dripped from his fingers. He tasted iron on his tongue.

A cry drew his attention. Enqi ran at full speed down a side street, leaping over corpses as he sprinted. After emerging in an adjacent plaza, he saw the airships had amassed high overhead here in the center of Sahael. Enil and Ninqi's forces continued to push back against the onslaught of legions, but casualties were obviously mounting.

"Attack! Show no mercy!" Great King Enil ordered.

Ninqi soared high on the back of Drake, helping destroy many of the smaller airships with the creature's powerful claws. The largest Airship shot an Obsidian hook that penetrated Drake's skin though, forcing him to dive back into the water of Sahael Lake. High King Ninqi swam to the shore and ordered his remaining forces to continue to fight to the last man.

King Sekhmet commanded the other half of his infantry to fight along with his bowmen and bow women, ordering them to attack the rest of the Narsans. They fired their turquoise-tipped arrows and took out hundreds as the Narsans moved into the city. He and his army charged into the fray, disappearing in smoke and rubble.

The sun had now fully set, and darkness reigned. Enough fires burned that it still seemed like midday in the city.

"Keep fighting!" Enqi cried as he decapitated two witans with a single strike. The Narsan forces had retreated yet again, but he knew another wave would hit soon.

"We can't hold them off any longer!" Ninqi said, waving his glowing blue sword over his head. "My cavalry is gone. Our remaining soldiers are confused and bleeding because of the aerial bombardment. We must return to the palace for a final stand. Send whoever remains through the Nairohenge Gates to safety!"

Great King Enil limped forward, supported by two of his generals. The entire right side of his body was burned, but he stood under his own power to address his fellow rulers.

"It's worse than you know," he said. "The Narsan army is passing back through the city enslaving everyone who hasn't been killed, even those who were witan due to the one-drop rule. They are placing them in mystic obsidian chains and cages that make them weak and tired. I also watched moments ago as King Sekhmet killed many Narsan infantrymen until he was struck with shrapnel from an explosion. His mount, the white rhino Rhilas, fled into the forest until he had healed himself. Sekhmet stood back up and continued fighting without his mount, but he was overcome. They tied up King Sekhmet, placed him on his knees, executing him in front of his men."

"No," Enqi whispered.

"I saw the Ennead too," Enil continued.

Ninqi's energy sword disappeared into thin air as if someone had blown out a candle. "Ennead? Here? Why?"

"They are collecting the dead," Enil confirmed. "They're being led by Atum himself. I received word he was seen on the grounds of Khartoum Palace."

"Commander-in-Chief Atum of the Ennead legion," Enqi breathed. The name brought fear among the soldiers almost as great as that of Natas himself.

Enil wiped blood from his chin. "He is in full command of the nine Ennead Legions whenever there's fresh death. The Ennead now have total and complete control over all death in Aarde. That right has apparently been taken away from the Demirrian people."

King Enqi didn't know what to do or think. He knew it was Sekhmet's people's responsibility to collect the dead, not the Ennead. If Atum's forces had indeed been granted that power by the gods, even the Educators of Timbuktu could have no power to overrule it.

And if the gods had made that decision, they knew that the sun had set on Sahael for the last time.

"How'd Commander in Chief Atum get into Khartoum Palace?" King Enqi asked quietly.

"He entered Necrosis's Chamber using Nebuchadnezzar's Chalcedony portal," Enil continued. "The navigators sent me word through NeRu's eyes. Commander-in-Chief Atum removed three coffins from the Necrosis Chamber; afterward the Chief dug several feet down into the ground and found Nzingha's obsidian key. Our time is at an end."

"But the battle isn't over," Enqi replied. "We haven't lost yet."

Enil's head dropped slightly. "Haven't we? The nine Ennead Legions are here dressed in exquisite black and gold Egyptus armor. There is no doubt they consider the battle over, and we are not the victors. They are using Njiru's nine Chalcedony rings to open Nebuchadnezzar portals and transport dead black and witan bodies to Naharis's realm."

"We must enter the palace and make sure the Nabtahenge

Gates retract into the ground safely so Natas can never use them," Ninqi said. "If we are to die tonight, Natas will have no prize." "I agree," Enqi nodded.

The three remaining kings ran back to Khartoum as fast as they could. Soldiers continued fighting all around them, but the more Enqi saw, the more he realized their cause was indeed lost. They charged through the front entrance of Khartoum Palace, directly to the center chamber and to the Nabtahenge Gates.

"Please get away from Sahael as far you can. Flee from this place," King Regent Enqi ordered the Medjay Gate Guardian and the Navigators.

The Medjay and the Navigators did as they were commanded and left as the Nairohenge Gates retracted into the ground.

Ninqi looked up at the painted ceiling a hundred feet above. This was a beautiful place. Generations had lived and ruled here. Kings and queens of old had sung and painted and eaten and loved under this roof.

But never again.

"Let us meet our enemy face-to-face," Ninqi said as he pointed toward the main entrance of the palace. "I wish to see Natas' red eyes and watch him bleed before the sun rises."

Nodding their heads, Enqi and Enil agreed. They walked shoulder-to-shoulder until they stood on the palace steps under the stars and waited for their doom.

They didn't need to wait long.

Soldiers marched toward Khartoum; Narsan, Ennead, and witan. There at their head stood Lord Commander Natas. His sevenfoot tall frame was at least a head taller than everyone else. Crimson tattoos glowed on his arms, making his dark brown skin appear instead dark red. His eyes glowed as well. Dreadlocks blew over his shoulder along with his dark cape. The air seemed to grow cold in his presence.

Natas walked through his men and stood at the base of the staircase leading to Khartoum Palace.

"My…" Natas paused, smiling. "…Kings."

Enqi, Ninqi, and Enil all formed their weapons simultaneously. The steps glowed in the light from Enqi's emerald blades, Ninqi's azure, and Enil's gray.

"Where is King Sekhmet?" Natas asked while picking at his fingernail. "Where are your queens and princesses? Where are your guards and soldiers? All dead already? It's only been two days, and yet here I stand on the steps of the great Khartoum Palace with the dead all around me. The Ennead now shepherd the dead where the Demirrian used to do it. It seems Alkebulan and Sahael are not what they once were."

"Shut your mouth, demon-made-flesh," High King Ninqi spat. "Ishtar and Obatala will never smile on you, no matter how much you wish for it."

Natas' face became hard with suppressed anger. "I am greater than Ishtar and Obatala. I am the way of life and death. I am all that is righteous." Natas took a deep breath. "Where are the queens and princesses? They should die with you here and now, swiftly, without pain. I am merciful to those who serve me."

Enqi looked at Ninqi and Enil. They had served as kings of Sahael together for decades. Their daughters had all been born on the same day, according to prophecy. Solomon had given a glimpse of death and suffering to Sekhmet, but also the potential for a unified future, so long as the princesses chose to bring it about.

Enqi nodded, not saying a word to his two friends...his brothers in arms. They all knew what this moment portended, and no words needed to be spoken.

A cry left Enqi's mouth as he leaped down the steps toward Natas, emerald sword slashing the air.

A smile flashed on Natas' lips for an instant before he formed a crimson sword in one hand and an ax in the other. Enqi's blade hit Natas' with a crack of lightning.

Ninqi and Enil joined the fight without hesitation. They swung their weapons as Natas blocked and parried. Enil tried to decapitate the man, but Natas ducked with speed that made the kings look slow in comparison. Natas sliced across Enil's stomach, opening a gash an inch deep. The High King stepped back and examined his would, but instantly jumped back into the fray.

Enqi leaped and dodged Natas' strikes, but Natas did the same, evading his opponents. The soldiers at the bottom of the steps stood silently watching as their Lord and Commander fought three men by himself. They seemed to enjoy the spectacle, never once doubting their master would be victorious.

Ninqi crouched, catching Natas off-guard and slicing the large man's leg just below the knee. It wasn't a deep cut, but it was enough to make Natas cry out in pain and surprise.

"You are no god!" Ninqi shouted for the surrounding soldiers to hear. "You bleed like a man, but you'll die like a rodent!"

Ninqi rushed forward, as did Enil, but Natas spun, tossing his glowing ax from behind, hitting Ninqi in the chest.

Enqi cried out, but it was too late.

The High King looked down at the energetic ax buried six inches deep in his sternum. He glanced slowly at Enqi and Enil before falling face-forward onto the steps. His headdress tumbled to the ground, resting among the stones.

The ax reformed in Natas' left hand. "Where are the princesses?!?" he bellowed, voice echoing throughout the courtyard. Rage took over as Enqi and Enil converged, attacking Natas from the right and the left. Again, Natas strafed back and forth, catching their blows with his weapons, and launching his own attack. He cut Enqi on the upper arm with his sword before slicing to the left and completely severing Enil's right hand from his wrist.

"Enil!" Enqi cried as the man's hand flopped against the steps.

Warm blood dripped down Enqi's bicep as he watched Enil reform his blade in his remaining left hand and charge at Natas. The two men smashed blades together, but Natas was too quick. Before Enqi could rejoin the fight, Natas stabbed Enil through the chest. Instead of stumbling back, however, Enil darted forward, smashing his forehead against Natas' nose. Natas stumbled back, wiping fresh blood from his upper lip.

"Bleed, demon," Enil coughed. The Great King looked at Enqi. "Have faith, my king brother…our daughters…will live to see…our land reclaimed…and Natas' final defeat. So, I…prophecy."

Enil collapsed and breathed no more.

While Natas was still distracted by his bloody nose, Enqi attacked once more. His twin swords swung with the speed of a cheetah. Natas responded with swipes of his own, but the two men found themselves unable to find an advantage over the other.

"I always wanted to face you in single combat, King Regent Enqi," Natas said between blows. "Your prowess in single combat is renowned. I supposed the fickle Sahaelian senate chose the right man to lead their armies after all."

Enqi screamed, blades slashing faster and faster. Natas responded in-kind.

Slowly over the next few minutes as the two men fought, Enqi felt his fatigue getting the better of him. Natas' blows became fiercer and faster, catching Enqi off-guard on several occasions and cutting the flesh of his arm and leg. Blood dripped freely onto the stone steps. Even so, Enqi moved like lightning, catching Natas offguard on several occasions, spilling the Lord Commander's blood as well.

Out of the corner of his eye, Enqi saw High Queen Nergal run up the steps behind Natas. She had two little girls in her arms and one on her back as she charged into Khartoum Palace.

Their daughters would survive. Enqi was sure of it.

That thought brought him comfort as Natas' hot red blade embedded itself in Enqi's stomach.

"Don't worry, King Regent Enqi," Natas whispered. "Your daughter and wife will join you in death soon enough. You've failed them. You've failed all of Sahael, Alkebulan, and Aarde itself. But don't fret, such was meant to be the moment I stepped foot in Timbuktu to seek my revenge."

Enqi dropped to his knees as Natas yanked the sword from his belly. Looking up, Enqi smiled.

"You are…a weak man, Natas," Enqi said as blood filled his mouth. "You believe it was prophesied…you would be victorious? Your victory will be but a moment…and someday my daughter, and the other princesses, will hold their boots to your neck as you beg for mercy."

Natas leaned closer to Enqi; teeth clenched. "Once you, the queens and princesses are all dead, I will destroy Nassir's sapphire obelisk that blesses the water here in Sahael. I will curse it so that no matter what magic you use, no matter how many gods rally to your side, Sahael will always be a dead land without a drop of water from Ouzoud's Waterfall. I will leave it a barren husk forever, so future generations will know what happens when Lord Commander Natas chooses an enemy.

Enqi smiled again and then spit blood in Natas' face.

The muscles in Natas' neck tightened as he stood up and held his ax to the side as if to slice perpendicular to the ground.

Enqi closed his eyes, knowing what was about to happen. He thought of Arishkegal and the afternoons they would walk together through the flowers in the Yoruban homelands. He thought of their wedding night and the birth of their daughter.

Aamira.

It would be up to her now, and the other princesses. They would hope to be successful in thwarting Natas. They would reunite the people of Alkebulan and heal Sahael from whatever Natas did to it.

Enqi had faith.

These thoughts passed through his mind as he felt a blade slice through the muscles and arteries of his neck. A strange breeze touched his face and he felt as if he were falling through space.

After that, King Regent Enqi felt no more.

# PART TWO: THE YORUBAN BLOODLINE

# CHAPTER I THE DIVERSION

Vannadale Colony, June 19th, The age of Enlightenment

The image of a severed head tumbling through the air filled Aamira's dreams before it seemed the entire world began to shake around her. Sweat dripped down her forehead and had drenched her pillow, bedsheets, and clothing.

"Aamira!" a whispered but forceful voice echoed. "Aamira, wake up!"

Braémah, Aamira's maidservant and caretaker since she was three years old, placed her hand over Aamira's mouth to keep her from crying out. The room was dark. Aamira could barely make out Braémah's careworn face or her long dreadlocks with their flecks of gray.

"Aamira," Braémah repeated, hand still on Aamira's mouth. "I need you to wake up right now, I'm going to remove my hand. Whatever you do, don't make sound. It's time to go. The rebellion started about a half hour ago. The barns on the south of the plantation are already ablaze."

The rebellion had already begun? Aamira rubbed her forehead. Things had moved too fast since she and her cousins Oadira and Heziarah had met the prophet Solomon after the Royal Rumble. Plans had been made for the slaves to rebel, yes, but not this soon. Not without Aamira having a chance to prepare.

She didn't feel prepared.

Delphine Lalaurie, Aamira's owner, and self-proclaimed 'protector' ran the largest slave sex trafficking ring in Eastern Aarde. She had kept Aamira in the luxurious mansion house for the past 15 years, trotting her out to show people the beautiful darkskinned woman that would fetch such a prize one day from a wealthy breeder. The estate itself consisted of over two thousand acres with a horse track, a small lake, and a smithing shop for helping produce obsidian chains to place on her slaves, preventing them from ever leaving her estate.

Delphine had resources Aamira could barely comprehend.

If Aamira tried to escape, as was the plan once the rebellion started, Delphine would be able to find her no matter how far she ran.

Aamira knew it.

She started to sweat even more. As was her habit, Aamira grabbed the decorative bracelet on her wrist and began twisting it back and forth. Only that and her ring remained from whatever life she had before the fall of Sahael, and it always gave her comfort in times of stress.

Right now, it didn't seem to be helping.

"Snap out of it and look me directly in the eyes," Braémah demanded of Aamira as if she was her mother.

Aamira let go of the bracelet and peered through the dark at the silhouette of the older woman.

"Stop playing with Nebiriau's bracelet and listen to me. We need to get you out of here as soon as possible," Braémah said. "The alarm hasn't been risen yet, but the riot will reach the main plantation houses within a few minutes. You'll never be able to escape after that."

Light caught Aamira's eyes through the window to her right. She ran over quickly and stared through the bars that kept her from ever escaping. She knocked over scented soapy water used for washing her clothes. It wasn't merely for hygiene's sake that such pleasures were afforded her. The hounds could smell the manure from a mile away and could track her easily if she was to ever run away.

"Dammit! We need a new set of unscented clothes for you again luckily, I've a second pair that you can use," Braémah said with frustration.

"Fire," Aamira said, pointing out the window. Through the orchard to the south, Aamira could see the light of flames from the storage barns.

"Help me get on some dry scentless clothes," Braémah whispered softly. She rummaged through one of the drawers and handed Aamira a cream-colored canvas shirt and coarse brown pants. "All of Madame Delphine's enslaved are rebelling and killing every witan on her estate; once we've got dressed, we need to get out of here before she comes back to the house looking for you in your room."

"Understood," Aamira said as she got dressed as quickly as she could. The clothes were scratchy against her skin. She had only worn them once before when Delphine was teaching her how to pick cotton and didn't want any snags on the fine dresses Aamira usually wore.

Screams started to echo in the night from far away but drawing closer with every second.

"Hurry, we need to leave now. The colonial militia will be here soon to stamp out this enslaved rebellion," Braémah said as they entered the hallway outside Aamira's room.

Madame Delphine's voice echoed through the downstairs, along with thumping footsteps of what Aamira assumed had to be plantation overseers.

"Gather up every enslaved female trying to sneak out of the house and bring them to the courtyard," Madame Delphine ordered. "Make sure Aamira is among them.

Terror suddenly gripped Aamira's heart. This had been her fear since the first time Solomon had visited her after the Royal Rumble with Nezikiah, the warrior pretending to impregnate Aamira and her cousins. Solomon had given her instructions on what to say to the slaves to get them to rebel, along with where she needed to go once she was free, but her mind had always focused on this moment; getting out of the house without being caught. Aamira had seen the slaves on the plantation beaten many times, but because of her worth to the madame as being pure and without blemish, Aamira had never suffered such depravities before.

Would she be beaten now? Would Delphine allow the overseers to rape her as they did many of the other women?

"Get to the second floor and find Aamira!" Delphine screamed.

"Yes, madame," one of the overseers said.

Aamira couldn't move. She stood against the wall trembling. If the house had suddenly caught fir, Aamira would burn right along with it, because her legs would not listen to her mind telling them to run.

"Come on!" Braémah said, grabbing Aamira by the shirt sleeve and pulling her to one of the side rooms where the laundry would be gathered.

"There's a shaft over here where we toss the laundry down to the first floor," Braémah said, kicking over a pile of dirty clothes. "There's also a rope ladder that leads down into the cellar of the house. Solomon warned me we may need alternative forms of escape, and I listened."

Aamira simply nodded as her heart pounded as if she had just run the entire length of the plantation. Braémah had listened intently to Solomon every time he had visited the plantation. It had been Braémah who had spoken to the slaves; Braémah who had planned. Aamira had spent her time trying to learn the magic artes

Solomon had taught her, but even now, months later, Aamira could barely form an energetic blade in her hand or communicate with animals. Everything had seemed so hard and impossible.

Why had the Gods chosen her and her cousins? It made sense that Oadira would be chosen. She was strong and angry. Heziarah had always been smart and cunning. But Aamira? She preferred the quiet of a good book. She didn't like talking to people, and the comfort of the mansion house had always been appreciated. Yes, people around her suffered, but did she need to suffer with them? It seemed needless.

And yet now here she was, the reason slaves were rebelling, thinking she was some great leader that would lead them to the mythic land of Sahael and be one of their queens. It was a fantasy, and Aamira knew it.

Footsteps pounded on the stairs down the hall.

Braémah helped Aamira lift the wooden hatch that covered the laundry chute. The rope ladder hung from the floor stretching down onto the ground.

"Follow me," Braémah said as they climbed down quickly into the main floor and opened a second hatch that had a rope leading to the cellar.

"She's not up here!" an overseer shouted from upstairs.

"God damn it!" Delphine shouted.

Aamira jumped. The voice had come from the adjoining room.

Delphine was right there.

If Aamira went out right now and begged for forgiveness, would Delphine be merciful? Would she forgive her?

Part of her wanted to take the first step toward the door and plead with Delphine to be forgiving.

"Come on!" Braémah urged as she once again grabbed Aamira's shirt and pulled her over to the rope. The two women quickly climbed down into the blackness of the cellar. Dust hung in the air and Aamira could smell dried pork and brined peaches. The room was pitch, save for a flickering light coming from one small window above Aamira's head at the level of the ground outside.

Fires had reached the orchard next to the house.

Aamira and Braémah rested for a moment before looking out the cellar window again at the chaos erupting everywhere. Buildings burned, enslaved men, women, and children ran away from hounds, overseers, and witans. People fell in the darkness outside, and Aamira couldn't tell whether they were slaves or slavers.

"It's getting worse out there, and madame Delphine will surely be looking for you," Braémah said. "Getting across the Estate in all of this confusion will be dangerous. We will trust in Solomon's council." Braémah placed her hand on Aamira's cheek. The light filtering through the small window reflected off a tear running down the old woman's face. "I've been taking care of you since you were three years old, and all your nightmares, dreams, and tremors from your childhood. I'll worry about you for the rest of my life as if you were my daughter. You're not my little girl anymore though, are you? You don't fall asleep on me as we read stories anymore…and you never will again."

"I'll be fine. Stop worrying about me," Aamira said.

She didn't believe it, even as the words left her mouth. Emotion roiled in Aamira's stomach. Trust in Solomon? Solomon wasn't here facing torture and death or being torn apart by bloodhounds and raped by witans.

"You're going to be okay," Braémah whispered. "I know that fear in your eyes, little one. I know you have no desire to run from your life. But listen to me now as you have never listened before. People are dying for you at this very moment out there. Men, women, and children. They're dying because they have hope for a better tomorrow, and they see you and your cousins as the key to that hope. You are not a child anymore. You are 18 years old. Are you going to let them down? Are you going to let them die because you're afraid and want a comfortable bed?"

Aamira shook her head. Shame filled her body like stones dropped from the sky. "No. I can be brave. I can trust Solomon."

"Good girl. Now, tell me your plan. Repeat it to me again just as Solomon told you so that it's clear in your mind."

"I need to find a way to get to the coast before daylight breaks," Aamira said rubbing her fingers into her moist palms.

"That's easier said than done and you know it, I taught you better than that," Braémah said candidly. "What did Solomon advise? Remember every word he spoke."

Shouts and footsteps thundered on the ceiling from the floor above.

"When I find those black heifers, I'm going to string them both by their toes," Madame Delphine yelled. "Check the cellar!"

"I can hear Madame Delphine! We have to go now," Aamira said desperately.

"There'd be no cover for us, we'll be out in the open exposed to the overseers, hounds, colonial militia, and the enslavement police catchers," Braémah warned, taking a deep breath.

"We need to get out of here now," Aamira exhaled. She ran to the cellar double doors and threw them open. The smell of smoke assaulted her nose. People ran here and there but Aamira didn't care. She needed to escape. She needed to run. She needed to avoid pain. Wind blew in her face as she charged into the night amid the shouts and screams of the carnage around her.

"Aamira! Wait!" Braémah yelled.

Looking behind her, Aamira watched as Braémah chased after her. Then she glanced movement in the shadow of the cellar entrance now 20 yards away. Madame Delphine, with her curled brownish-gray hair, pointed at Aamira and shouted something.

Aamira's feet never stopped pumping. She focused back in front of her, looking at the trees of the grove drawing closer. She could lose them in the grove.

A dog barked to her left suddenly, followed by a searing pain in her thigh.

"Ahhh!!" yelled Aamira as she hit the ground.

"Stop it, you damned beast!" Braémah screamed as the hound's teeth tore into Aamira's leg.

Braémah picked up a rock and smashed it into the dog's head. A whimper filled the night air as the dog released Aamira's thigh and ran off.

Aamira stood back up, shakily as pain tore at her mind. Still, the need to reach the trees overcame any agony she could have felt.

"Help me up. I'll be okay," Aamira said, wincing in pain with each step she took.

The two women limped to the grove as quickly as they could and didn't stop until the sounds of chaos were muffled by the leaves and trunks of oak trees.

"Oh, my child we have to get you somewhere safe before the hounds, and the overseers get a hold of you," Braémah said, ripping cloth from her dress and making a bandage to cover the wound on Aamira's leg. "You're lucky the dog only got a chance to sink its teeth in. I've seen these beasts tear the flesh clean off when they're biting and raging. They'll be able to smell the blood though. We need to keep moving. We got lucky."

"I can hear the hounds in the distance," Aamira said, sweat dripping from her nose.

They were done for. This entire escape was doomed to failure. Why had Aamira listened to Solomon? Only one thing she knew was that she didn't want Braémah to come to harm.

"It's time for you to save yourself," Aamira said, wincing as she leaned against a large oak. "They're looking for me. Madame Delphine will be mad at me, but she'll understand. They'll kill you for this though. I'll stay here and wait for them. You can escape."

Braémah chuckled. "You have courage you don't understand, Aamira. I wish I could live to see it blossom."

"What are you talking about?" Aamira asked breathlessly. It was clear Braémah wasn't planning to escape.

"The forest circles to the south," Braémah continued. "Head in that direction and I will draw Madame Delphine, the overseer, and the Lope hounds in my direction. It's the only way, my child."

"But they'll catch you," Aamira said, placing her hands on both of Braémah's shoulders.

"Shh, they're getting close and will hear us, get to the desert sand lands of IFF as quickly as you can. You'll be safe when you arrive, just as Solomon promised," Braémah whispered, covering Aamira's mouth with her right hand.

Shouts and barks grew closer in the forest. Aamira could practically smell the perspiration of the greasy overseers.

"We have to split up to save you," Braémah said, glancing over her shoulder toward the sound. "I'm going to head East and North. You keep heading South. This is the only way to get you off this island. The rest will take care of itself. Find the Marula Trees. They will help heal you on your way to the ships. Follow

Solomon's plan." Braémah hugged Aamira and kissed her on the cheek. "On the count of three, we move in opposite directions."

"I don't want to leave you," Aamira cried. Her chest heaved with a sob loud enough for anyone around to hear.

"Promise me, you won't stop until you reach the Sand Lands of IFF," Braémah urged, face serious. "I know you, child. I know you haven't taken all of this seriously. You wasted much of your time with Solomon over the past few months. Promise me you'll make it to IFF. Promise!"

"I…promise."

"Good. Now, one, two, three," Braémah said, darting away from Aamira toward the shouted voices.

On instinct, Aamira charged in the opposite direction. Leaves crunched under her feet as she ran. The pain in her leg ached, but she barely noticed as the trees flew by in her periphery. Muscles burned throughout her body. Each breath she took constricted her chest in ragged gasps.

*I need to find somewhere to hide,* Aamira thought to herself.

After what she assumed had to have been at least several miles of running, Aamira saw something that caught her eye. In the pale moonlight, she saw a grove of Marula Trees. She hadn't known there were any Marulas on the island were p\growing, and yet here they were. Solomon had mentioned Marulas being a protection for her during her journey, and Braémah had reiterated it just before running off.

Was this a sign? Should she hide here or keep running?

As she slowed down and walked through the grove, she noticed one of the Marula Trees had an opening in the trunk that was large enough for a person to squeeze into. If she chose to hide, this would be as good a place as any.

Making a decision, Aamira pushed her way into the opening in the trunk and found a rather spacious opening inside that was enough for her to spread out and lean into the folds of the tree. Insects scurried over her feet as if searching for the blood from her wound. The pain intensified now that she was no longer running. Sweat dripped from her brow and she wanted nothing more than to embrace oblivion for a little while. The smooth bark felt cool against her skin as she took deep breaths and closed her eyes.

Aamira awoke with a start, not having realized she had fallen asleep. The sky beyond the tree hollow grew lighter, but dawn was still an hour away at least. She heard nothing except her heartbeat.

As she continued resting, muffled voices suddenly filled the night air. She sat up and peered through the opening in the trunk, seeing a group of seven escaped slaves; black men, women, and children, being pursued by hounds and slave-catching police. Aamira listened to the bloodhounds coming from another direction knowing the family would be killed for running away.

Aamira had listened to many conversations over the years involving Madame Delphine and her uppity, stupid witans who considered themselves the upper echelon of society. They would show no mercy to people like this family. They would murder innocents and pat themselves on the back afterward.

*They need my help,* Aamira thought, as the runaways drew closer to the Marula Tree. *I can't leave them to fend for themselves.*

Aamira made a decision. There was enough room in the hidden chamber of the tree for at least six more people. If they squished, all of them could fit.

"Get inside quickly! You'll be safe inside of this Marula Tree," Aamira said, hand waving through the opening to draw their attention.

"Princess Aamira?" one of the women asked.

Princess Aamira. There was nothing Aamira considered royal about herself, and the fact that the slaves called her that made her incredibly uncomfortable.

"It's okay, get inside. You can trust me," Aamira said waving her arms signaling the runaways to enter. "I promise, it's safe. Hurry!"

The runaways quickly entered the Marula Tree one by one taking deep breaths. They fell to their knees from exhaustion, fatigue, and hunger. To her surprise, Aamira found there was more space than she thought inside the hollow. She expected them to be smooshed together, but they all had their own space.

*It must have been a trick of the darkness,* she thought.

Soon the sounds of dogs and slave catchers grew louder. At one point, a hound came up to the tree and sniffed loudly, but then ran off when called by its master. Quickly, quietness returned to the grove as the slavers ran off in search of their quarry.

The runaways sighed in relief.

"How did they not smell us?" the same woman who spoke previously asked.

"I don't know," Aamira admitted. "Tell me your names."

The people pointed at their mouths with their fingers and exposed their mouths and tongues to Aamira.

"These people all had their tongues cut out by Delphine

Lalaurie to get them to fall in line," the woman said. "Only Abioye here, and myself, can still speak. I was bringing them to the shore, but we were going to be caught and needed somewhere to hide. Seeing you here inside of the Marula Tree was the perfect place where I knew these people would be safe. I am Reilish."

"How have you come to know about his location?" Abioye, a young man about Aamira's age who stood seven tall with dreadlocks, a chiseled, muscular frame, and ivory teeth, asked. "My maidservant Braémah told me to find the Marula Trees," Aamira replied. "Solomon had mentioned the same thing. I found this hollow tree a few hours ago. What time is it, do you think?"

"Almost dawn," Abioye answered. "It will be light soon."

"Braémah and several other enslaved women planted these Marula Trees over 15 years ago," Reilish said, rubbing her hand against the bark. "They said they were preparing for the day of the great rebellion. Whether they will help anyone else, I do not know, but they certainly helped us this night." She looked down at Aamira's leg. "You are wounded. I see blood on the bandage." Aamira touched her thigh. Since waking up, the wound hadn't bothered her in the slightest. She had all but forgotten about it.

"I was wounded by one of the dogs, but…" She removed the strip of cloth and felt her leg. No remnant of the bite remained.

She had been healed.

Reilish smiled and looked around at the gathered group. "I told you she was one of the sovereigns that would save our people. I told you!"

The slaves nodded excitedly.

Aamira didn't want to be worshiped or fawned over. She wanted to escape and survive.

"Braémah told me to do whatever I can to get off this island and to the ships departing to the desert lands of IFF," Aamira explained as she looked down to the ground.

"Wonderful! We're looking to get to the ships heading to the desert lands as well," Abioye said, eyes slanted as if looking to see Aamira's reaction.

"I need to get the Sand Lands of IFF as quickly as possible," Aamira repeated. She didn't know what else to say. Was the young man trying to test her in some way? That's how she had always felt about Solomon; he pushed her to do things she didn't want to do.

"Do you know the way to the docks?" Abioye asked.

"No. Only that they are to the south. Solomon told me, but I…" She wanted to say, 'I never believed the rebellion would happen, so I didn't pay close attention,' but instead blurted, "I don't know anything beyond that."

"We know the way," Reilish nodded. "My late husband used to run carts from the plantation to the ships."

"You can come with us. I'll help you get there," Abioye said calmly.

"Then what's the plan?" Aamira asked.

"There's a lot to consider," Abioye replied. "I know you're scared, but just trust that I have everyone's best interests in mind. Let's allow the people to rest for several hours first. Once the sun has risen, we'll move through all the chaos and blend in with the other enslaved that have run away who are traveling to the Vannadale shores."

"We all need to stay close to each other," Aamira nodded.

As Abioye spoke, Nebiriau's bracelet lit up, casting a green glow around the hollow.

"What is that?" Reilish asked, face lit up in the brightness.

"It's Nebiriau's bracelet," Aamira answered, looking at the faces around her and seeing their details for the first time. Many scars were evident in the light, that the darkness had hidden. "It was given to me by my mother before her death."

"Abioye is my name," Abioye said. "We all know your name, Princess Aamira. Braémah told us you are a princess of Sahael and will lead our people to freedom." He looked at Reilish. "Maybe you're right about all of this."

The glow diminished, leaving the group in darkness once more. Abioye watched the bracelet as it dimmed. Aamira trusted him. He seemed to be confident and know what he was doing. For the first time since getting woken by Braémah, Aamira felt calm.

The sky began to lighten slowly as dawn approached.

"We should move now before it grows any lighter," Abioye said, walking toward the crevice in the tree. He peered out and nodded. "I don't hear anything. No dogs barking or voices. If we run, we should be able to reach the docks quickly."

Aamira, Abioye, and the group of enslaved runaways left the crevice of the Marula Tree and started charging south. Day broke as they journeyed. Smoke lingered on the air as an overcast sky looked down on them. Occasionally they would find a dead body in the forest; a slave or a militiaman bloodied and cold.

Looking over her shoulder at the group behind her, Aamira paid close attention to the two young children: a boy, and a girl. Scars ran up their backs and the boy had a bruise over his left eye. They couldn't have been older than ten or eleven.

Aamira shut her eyes for a moment as they ran through the trees. She wanted to cry. Were these children better off now, running for their lives through the forest, or back at the plantation where they would be oppressed and beaten?

Was Aamira better off now, running for her life through the forest, or back at the plantation where she was comfortable, but worth no more to her mistress than what she would bring in a dowry?

Aamira didn't know the answer.

As they approached the outskirts of the coastal villages, the carnage intensified until they heard the sounds of pitched battle.

"What's happening?" Aamira asked as she heard screams and saw a house burning just through the trees.

"The rebellion has reached the coast," Abioye said. "The Vannadale colonial militia has arrived. I can't see much from here, but it looks like our rebelling brothers and sisters have started bringing the fight to the militia. Soon the Vikings will be released on the witans looking for Valhalla and join in this rebellion." Abioye grinned from ear to ear. "Let's move between the houses and see if we can reach the docks."

"No ships will be sailing during a pitched battle," Reilish whispered. "They've either already sailed, or they're on fire right now."

Would they be trapped here? Would Aamira be caught? Would she be punished for running away? Her heart pounded, and not from the last two hours of running.

Abioye looked back into the forest, biting his lower lip. "Let's find a place to hide for now in the village. If the ship to IFF is gone already, we'll figure something out. We can't stay here. Maybe we can find an abandoned house and at least a morsel of food for the children."

The bloodshed on both sides was gruesome as the group slinked through the town. Corpses littered the streets and yards of the town. Many homes and businesses burned. The battle seemed to have receded from this area however, and Aamira followed Abioye as he turned down an alley between two brick shops.

"These are General Scipio's men," Reilish said as they stepped over a decapitated soldier wearing a gray uniform with a blue cape.

"How can you tell?" Abioye asked.

"The cape," Reilish answered. Her face was hard as granite, as if she hated the dead man lying in the alley.

"Let's go," Abioye urged.

A few minutes later, they had made their way to the outskirts of town where they found a large two-storied estate house with white shutters and a red brick façade. Several witan bodies lay in the blood-stained grass.

"Can we stop here?" Aamira asked. Her legs were tired, and she was hungry. Glancing back at the two children, she could only imagine what they were feeling. "This mansion looks empty. It will allow us time to rest and leave again when the skies darken once more." Her bracelet lit up again for a moment.

Abioye glanced at the bracelet. "Let's check it out. We may be safe here for the daylight to pass and start traveling once again under the cover of night."

They snuck around back and found several more dead bodies. Abioye opened the back door, and they entered a dark pantry area with shelves and stores of preserved fruits and pickled vegetables in jars. The area had been partially ransacked though, with several broken bottles on the floor, mingled with juices and squishy peaches. It smelled like vinegar and syrup.

Someone whispered in the darkness beyond the pantry, and a chair scraped against the floorboards.

Abioye stepped forward and peered into the shadowed room.

"It's okay," he said, turning back to Aamira.

The group entered a large kitchen area with wood-burning stoves, serving tables and chopping blocks. At least 20 escaped slaves filled the space, eating directly from the jars. Most of them were older, with a few children mixed in. Their thin and weak bodies trembled, either from hunger or fear.

"It's alright," Abioye said, arms raised as if to tell them he meant no harm. "We're just here to hide, like you."

The hiding slaves welcomed them, sharing the preserves gladly as if Aamira and her entourage were family. Aamira ate greedily from a jar of peaches, enjoying the sweet nectar. She watched as the older slaves allowed the younger to eat first, so the children could be satisfied. They smiled, so grateful to have the jars of food. It was as if this was the greatest meal they had ever enjoyed.

A deep shame twisted Aamira's gut as she ate the last of her peaches and placed the jar on the wood floor next to where she sat. She had never considered herself a slave; not like those who served in the fields. And yet here she was with them, understanding for the first time what their lives were truly like. She had never gone hungry. Sure, she hated not being able to make her own choices, and she hated the overseers and how they treated people, but all of that hate had always been from a safe distance.

She understood how the slaves had lived, but from a safe distance.

Tears dripped down her cheeks in the dark room.

Where was Oadira right now? Oadira, so brave and smart. She was probably fighting alongside the slaves on her plantation, killing witans and rescuing children. Where was Heziarah, headstrong and stubborn? Probably charging through legions of soldiers all by herself, conquering and bringing peace.

And where was Aamira?

Crying in a mansion by the sea, eating peaches while children starved.

"I'll keep first-watch while everyone rests," Abioye said, pulling Aamira back to the present. "A couple of us have searched the house and no one else is here. From the upstairs windows we can see everything. The battle has moved along the coast to the east, and it looks like all the ships are still docked. We can see the masts over the rooftops. Stay inside, and as night falls, get as comfortable as you can."

Eventually, night fell, and the dark house grew pitch. Silence reigned. Aamira remained in the same place in the kitchen where she had spent most of the day. Breathing and snoring filled the room, but Aamira was unable to sleep. She decided to keep watch with Abioye.

The stairs creaked under her feet as she entered the second floor and found Abioye sitting in an opulent bedroom in a rocking chair, staring out on the night. Fires burned in the distance, but around the estate, all was quiet.

"Shouldn't you be getting rest? You're a highly valued slave treated like royalty," Abioye said, no emotion to his voice.

"What's that supposed to mean?" Aamira asked as she folded her arms.

"You know exactly what it's supposed to mean," Abioye said sharply.

"No, I don't know what it means. Care to enlighten me?" Aamira said, tapping her foot and moving her head from side to side.

"No need," Abioye said.

"So much for me thanking you getting us to the coast," Aamira said snidely.

"You're most welcome," Abioye replied.

Aamira wanted to throw something hard at Abioye as she looked around the dark room.

"I'm not trying to be something special," Aamira mumbled after her search for something to throw came up empty. "I never promised anything to anyone."

"That's the point," Abioye said, still staring out the window. "When Braémah would come to talk to us about the rebellion, telling everyone about Solomon teaching you and that you would lead us, I was skeptical, and I wasn't alone. But we trusted Braémah. She was an Educator of old, and always knew things we didn't. When we met you in the tree hollow, I thought maybe I'd been wrong and that you would lead us. Once we arrived here though, and you didn't even tell anyone who you were, I knew I had been right all along."

Aamira sat on the bed. The soft comforter reminded her of her own bedroom. "I'm sorry I'm not what you expected. I'm not what I expected either. I'm starting to realize I kept myself too distant from everything going on at the plantation." She looked over her shoulder toward the open door and the people sleeping downstairs. "I know I need to understand things better. Tell me about the people downstairs. You were speaking with one of them most of the afternoon."

"They are all traumatized, frightened, and scared, not wanting to move out of fear that one among their group could possibly turn them in," Abioye said.

"Turn them in?" Aamira asked.

"Yes," Abioye said. "Witan supremacy has infected their minds, forcing many to turn on their own kind after they've run away. Don't tell me you haven't thought about it since we left; the opportunity of going back and having everything you want? Now imagine that for people who have never known anything but suffering, and suddenly getting the chance to have the comforts you've always enjoyed. The witans call it a disease when the Blacks run away from their estates. Drapetomania. witans will make up anything to spread and sustain their supremacy over any group of people; especially Black people."

Aamira nodded. She had heard the term before while sitting with Madame Delphine during dinners with the other estate owners. They would laugh and Delphine would say something like, *"Aamira understands. She's one of the good ones. She knows we're speaking the truth."*

They sat in silence for a while. Aamira could smell the smoke from the fires in the distance. She could have died today. It was the first time she had ever felt that kind of fear…the fear these slaves felt all the time.

"I share those same thoughts and opinions sometimes," Aamira admitted. "What you said about Drapetomania. The overseers would talk about it. I started believing it was real." "Is that so?" Abioye asked.

"Yes," Aamira said. "If we're being honest, I should be honest. We all nearly died today, after all. You don't have to be a witan to practice witan supremacy."

"Are you're just understanding that now?"

"I'm starting to understand a lot of things for the first time."

Again, they sat in silence for a time. Wind blew in from the open window, cool and pleasant, with only a hint of ash.

"Sometimes the mental chains of whiteness and supremacy are the hardest ones to break," Abioye nodded.

"Where's Reilish?" Aamira asked. "I didn't see her with the other escaped slaves when I came up here."

“She is in the cellar with a group of women who didn’t want to be with everyone else. Reilish is kind and motherly. She knew how to comfort them when I didn’t.”

Abioye leaned forward in the rocking chair and focused on the horizon.

“What are you looking for?” Aamira asked. Abioye’s eyes had not moved from the horizon, as if he searched the night for something specific.

“I sent out a few of the young men an hour ago to spy and see what was happening at the ships. Hopefully they’ll return shortly with word on what movement occurs there. From here it looks like none of the ships have sailed yet, but with the rebellion, I can’t imagine they’re going to wait any longer. I need to know if the vessel sailing to IFF is still here and when it plans to sail.”

“Tell me more about this group,” Aamira continued.

Abioye took a deep breath, eyes still focused on the fires. “The group consisted of old women, young women, and little girls who were all involved in sex trafficking. When they noticed Nebiriau’s bracelet on your wrist, they all let their guard down.”

Aamira’s bracelet shined brightly as if acknowledging Abioye’s words.

Suddenly an ache filled Aamira, but instinctively she knew this anxiety and fear didn’t belong to her. Aamira could feel the pain and trauma in the bodies of the women downstairs. The thumps of their beating hearts and the anguish they felt coursed through the bracelet and into Aamira’s heart. It was as if she herself had let an emotional wall come down and the bracelet took advantage. Aamira knew they needed to help these people, but she just didn't know how. She had already asked Abioye for help to get her to the coast, and now she wanted to ask him for more of his support to help the women who had been forced into trafficking.

Aamira took a deep breath as the emotions she felt decreased with the bracelet's glow.

"You're going to ask me to help these people as well, aren't you?" Abioye asked.

Aamira nodded in agreement.

"No," Abioye stated.

"We need to help these women and little girls; we need to take them with us; if we leave them, they'll be caught and killed," Aamira said, looking Abioye directly in his eyes with confidence. "If they remain here, they'll eventually be caught, killed, or worse; forced to enter the trade once more."

Abioye looked at Aamira with confusion and frustration, putting his hands up in the air. "Do you know what happens when a rebellion is quelled?"

"No," Aamira admitted.

"When a rebellion happens, the colonial militia are ordered by General Scipio to kill everyone, once it has stopped. Every man, woman, and little child will be killed to prevent the idea from entering into the minds of the newly trafficked girl, boy, man and woman to prevent future rebellions."

Abioye stood from the chair and began slowly pacing back and forth.

In that moment, Aamira wished she could go back in time and do things differently. She wished she could return to her lessons with Solomon and pay more attention to everything he taught. She wished she had practiced her magic artes more diligently. She wished she had done more to help the people suffering on Delphine's plantation.

She couldn't change the past, but she could help now.

"If we take them with us, Ishtar and Obatala will bless our path," Aamira said slowly. "One thing I remember Solomon telling me was that the gods help those who help others. Maybe that's why I'm so weak when it comes to using my abilities, because I never tried to help anyone." Aamira's back straightened as Abioye stopped pacing and looked at her for the first time since she entered the room. "I can't change the past, but I can choose differently now than I would have then. You don't have to help us if you don't want to, but I won't abandon these people. I'll die with them if I have to." Aamira hadn't realized what she'd said until she said it. Would she die with them? In that moment, she believed she would, and that would have to be enough.

The edges of Abioye's lips pulled up slightly. He nodded and folded his arms.

"They can follow us," he said. "We will find a way to protect them and get them on the ships as well. It's the least we can do for these children," Abioye said. "You should go get some rest. The young men I sent out should return shortly and we can---"

Shouts from the streets below rang through the night, along with the barking of dogs.

A group of enslaved men and young boys ran from a pack of Lope Mastiffs. Thc Lopes were large, four-foot-tall dogs as big as horses with the ability to smell from over two hundred miles away. One of the dogs pounced on a young man and bit the back of his neck as the lad screamed.

"We have to help them," Aamira said, stepping toward the door.

Abioye grabbed her arm as more screamed and filled the night.

"No," he whispered. "Those are the boys I sent out. If they've been tracked, we'll have to wait to move."

"We should intervene and save them," Aamira said, ready to jump out of the window and start fighting if needed. The cries of the boys tore at her heart.

"We can't!" Abioye said more forcefully, pulling Aamira closer to him. "The witans will have lookouts watching their movement just in case they're ambushed. If we attack them, we put all these people in danger."

Aamira didn't like Abioye's response. "That's not a good enough reason."

"And you need to grow the hell up!" Abioye hissed. "This is life and death we're dealing with; you live, or you die. It's that simple. This is a world the rest of us have been living in our entire lives. I've been trying to protect the people around me since I was four years old. What have you been doing? Getting your hair done and wearing fancy dresses? If you want to save them, go ahead, but I won't be helping you at all. Do what you have to do, you spoiled little brat!"

Abioye walked out of the room.

The cries and whimpering echoed through the night as the slavers tied up their quarry and dragged them back up the road.

Aamira tried to conjure a blade in her hand, but the green light flickered, taking the shape of a knife, but never becoming fully solid.

Abioye had been right. There was nothing she could do to help the boys. If she wanted to be of use now, she would need to do what Solomon had told her in the first place. She needed to realize she was a queen, blessed with abilities meant to serve other people, not herself. She couldn't doubt or think for one second, she couldn't accomplish the unimaginable.

The bedsprings squeaked as Aamira sat down. Closing her eyes, she focused on her hand, calling the power from her mind and body. A pale light glowed between her fingers as she concentrated.

She would manifest a blade if it took the rest of the night.

Nothing would stop her ever again.

Especially her own fear and doubt.

# CHAPTER II

# A BONDED AWAKENING

Vannadale Colony, June 20th, The age of Enlightenment

A cock crowed in the distance and Aamira awoke on the bed. Sunlight came through the open window, lighting the room.

She had practiced until exhaustion had taken her. Only once during her training had she successfully manifested a weapon. Still, it was better than nothing.

Footsteps thumped against the floorboards in the hallway.

"We have to go, now," Abioye said as he stepped into the room. "One of the scouts I sent out returned a few minutes ago. He was able to escape the hunters last night. The ships are all sailing away in the next few hours. The battle hasn't gone well for the colonial forces apparently, and the ships are abandoning the port without even waiting for the rest of their cargos to arrive."

"We need a plan," Aamira said as she jumped up from the bed.

"We hide in the trees that surround this place, and travel safely to the docks," Abioye said as Aamira followed him into the hallway and down the stairs. "We have to move fast. I don't know what patrols are still out, but we have to risk it."

Aamira and Abioye entered the back kitchen where dozens of escaped slaves crammed. It seemed like even more had joined the group in the night. Reilish shepherded the group, telling everyone to follow Abioye and Aamira and that everything would be alright. They listened to the older woman, trusting in her wisdom.

"Abioye and the princess will keep us safe," Reilish told the gathering. "Don't worry. We will escape!"

Aamira wished she had the kind of faith Reilish had cultivated. The woman reminded her of Braémah; unstoppable, intelligent, and courageous.

Where was Braémah now? Had she escaped the slavers? Had she been captured? The thought of Braémah being tortured made Aamira's stomach churn. She prayed in that instant that her mentor and friend, the closest thing she'd ever had to a mother, had escaped and was safe.

Abioye led the slaves into the forest behind the estate and ran toward the dock. To their surprise, they were immediately spotted by enslavement catchers, who started pursuing them violently.

"Catch those black bastards now!" a greasy man with missing teeth screamed as he set several dogs loose after the runaways. The beasts immediately ripped into the slowest members of the gathering. Shouts and pained cries reached Aamira's ears as she charged forward with Abioye, passing trees and jumping over bushes.

Heart pounding, the edges of Aamira's vision began to blur. The faster they ran, the more a headache grew from behind her eyes. Dizziness intensified and for a moment, Aamira feared she would fall over and pass out. The bracelet on her wrist burned her skin, pulsating with great intensity. Like the night before, Aamira felt the fear and anxiety of the escaped slaves. Their emotions became her own, and it was too much.

"Are you alright?" Aamira heard Abioye ask, but her vision seemed to be darkening to a pinpoint and sound came from far away.

What was happening? Was she tired from her practice the night before? Had conjuring blades taken more out of her than she realized? Or was something else wrong with her?

"This isn't good," Aamira said to Abioye. She slowed down and leaned against a tree. The world swayed back and forth.

"They're going to catch us," Abioye said.

The rest of the slaves gathered around, some asking if Aamira was alright. Everyone looked around terrified, ready for dogs and killers to jump out of the trees and grab them.

Abioye looked around frantically. "We can't wait here! We all need to hurry and hide behind the Marula Trees."

Aamira knelt down and then collapsed onto the ground. Dry leaves crunched against her body. The cool ground, still moist from the morning dew, seemed to embrace her. She could hear the whispers of the people around her. Some of them thought they should leave her behind; others said she was a princess and they needed her to survive.

"What are you doing?" Abioye asked, voice all but panicking.

A deep breath filled Aamira's lungs. Touching the ground made her headache vanish. She thought she could hear the roots of the trees around her digging into the soil. Whispered words became shouts in her mind, as if the ground amplified every word. *"She's slowing us down! The dogs will be on us at any moment!"*

*"Someone pick her up. We can't stay here."*

*"Give our princess a moment,"* Reilish chided.

*"Find them! Let the Mastiffs loose! We won't lose these niggers!"*

The last whisper came from some distance away, but Aamira heard it as though the man stood next to her. In fact, she could tell exactly where the voice originated. It was a half mile north in a thick area of brambles. The man had three dogs with him, and four other men.

They were moving toward them, slowly, through the thickets.

Aamira couldn't have that. She couldn't have these men find them.

The earth itself wanted to help. She could feel it. Never before had Aamira felt a connection like this. The soil, trees, and rocks offered their aid. She couldn't have explained it with words if she had been asked to describe the sensation.

During one of their training sessions, Solomon had told her that Aarde itself was her ally, and to trust its wisdom. She hadn't understood what he had meant and asked no further questions. Was this what the prophet wanted her to know?

Aamira rolled onto her stomach and raised to her knees, shakily. Leaning forward, she dug her fingers into the dirt.

"What's she doing?" somcone asked.

Eyes closed, Aamira focused on the voices of the men and dogs a half mile away. She needed to slow them down even more than the brambles were. She needed them to be afraid.

The earth itself knew what to do. Aarde answered her thoughts with a slight trembling around her. The ground shook. Pebbles danced against vibrating leaves. Several slaves gasped. The shockwave roiled through the ground and shot in the direction of the slave hunters. By the time it reached them, Aamira could feel its power increase. The world shook around the men. The dogs yelped and scattered. The hunters fell to their knees in terror.

"What was that trembling?" a woman whispered.

"It came from the princess," another replied.

"Help her up, Abioye" Reilish commanded.

"Aamira get up!" Abioye said, grabbing Aamira by the arm. "We don't have much time. The police, and their Lope Mastiffs are going to see us out here in the open."

Standing weakly, Aamira slumped against Abioye, exhausted beyond anything she had ever felt before. "It's…okay," she gasped. "The hunters…are afraid now. We have…time. Keep…moving."

"Are you okay? Abioye asked.

"Yes, just…weak," Aamira answered.

"What did you do, princess?" a young girl asked, tugging on Aamira's tattered shirt.

"I don't know," Aamira replied. "I was…feeling and hearing everything in this patch of forest. I could see and hear the movements of the enslavement catchers, the colonial militia, and the police. They're all in the forest looking for us, but Aarde wanted to help. I…I don't know what I did. The ground shook and then moved toward them. They ran away."

Everyone looked at Aamira with a mix of awe and fear. "Your eyes have changed color," Abioye said, staring at Aamira.

"What do you mean, they've changed color?"

"They're now emerald," Abioye replied. "They were dark brown like ours, but after you put your hands into the dirt, they changed. How is that possible?"

"The signs of the times are upon us!" Reilish shouted.

"The signs of the times are upon us!" the crowd cheered.

"Shut up!" Abioye cried. "What do you think you're all doing? Be quiet, for Ishtar's sake! Now start running! Go! We can't wait here anymore." No one moved.

No one spoke.

They all looked to Aamira as if Abioye hadn't spoken.

"What happened, princess?" the little girl asked.

"I wish I knew," Aamira answered, thinking about what Solomon had told her and her cousins in his tent outside of the coliseum. He said they had power beyond their expectations. For the first time, Aamira was understanding what he had meant. If only she had paid more attention to his counsel when she had the chance.

"Lead us, princess," a man said, stepping forward. Other slaves followed, crushing closer to her as if she carried the key to their salvation.

Aamira looked at Abioye. The young man seemed terribly confused. Moments before, he had been the leader. Now, the people were abandoning him without so much as a 'thank you.' As she looked at him, Aamira felt the rings on her fingers vibrate slightly.

Who was Abioye? He was strong and handsome, but there was something else there Aamira couldn't understand.

“Lead us, our princess,” Reilish said, repeating the words being whispered throughout the gathering.

Abioye glanced over his shoulder at the slaves and then nodded his head, as if giving Aamira permission to take over.

“Okay,” she began slowly. “Getting to the shore needs to be our priority. Abioye knows the way, so we will follow him. Everyone stay together and leave no one behind.”

“The ships will be leaving soon,” Abioye said, picking up where Aamira left off. “Follow me. And like Aamira said, stick together and make sure to help any stragglers.”

Abioye, Aamira, and the group traveled through the forest for another twenty minutes, making their way down a ravine and into the small town surrounding the docks. Brick buildings surrounded them. Some of the windows were broken, but none of the buildings had been burned.

“We’re here,” Abioye said with relief.

“We made it,” Aamira whispered under her breath, taking a deep sigh and patting Abioye on his back.

They made their way to the harbor, where thousands of people swarmed. Ships swayed in the current as sails dropped from their riggings to catch the breeze. Witan military men herded captured slaves with their swords and spears. Captains shouted from the causeway about getting underway before the battle turned back toward the docks.

Aamira and the group watched from an alleyway as bloodied and chained slaves were pushed frantically toward three different ships. Most of the slaves were old and gray, but some had obviously been captured during the battle and were being forced out to sea as well. Hundreds of broken down men and women who were young but looked old, stumbled by in obsidian chains. Their skin was leathery and beat up with hundreds of scars and deep unhealed flesh wounds all over them. Many of them had deformities and were hunched over due to years of hard labor.

They had been treated like chattel without rights, seen as only property and as three fifths of a person per witan decree. They were now being given away with only several months to live, hunted like beasts for the enjoyment of the cruelest people humanity could offer.

"They look like the walking dead," Aamira said, shocked. The slaves from Delphine's plantation looked robust and strong compared to these poor people.

"Typically, the broken enslaved are sent here to the coast to die in the Desert Sand Lands of IFF," Abioye said. "The witans find it economically more feasible to hunt the old as practice for their military and the Dalean people. Once the enslaved are worked to death and their bodies, minds, and health have started declining at a rapid rate, the slavers use them for sport. There are enough young slaves here that we should be able to blend in with them and pass through the standard checkpoints and inspections."

Abioye turned to the gathering behind him and instructed everyone to stay close together, but to mingle with the crowd.

"Make your way toward the *Ephebell*," Abioye ordered. "That's the ship headed to IFF. Everyone, smear dirt, mud, moss, whatever you can find, on your faces and any exposed skin. I know we're all pretty dirty already, but we need to look even worse to blend in with these people. Go!"

Reilish wandered quickly through the group, passing along where to go and how to act among the other slaves. Aamira bent down and grabbed some mud beside a trough of water used by horses. She smeared the muck on her face, arms, and clothing. The cool mud felt good on her skin after the sprint from the estate house, but she knew it would soon harden and become uncomfortable.

As soon as a contingent of old and weary black men and women wandered close to the building, Abioye slowly shepherded the escapees into the crowd.

Aamira shuffled her feet, head hanging low, and mingled among the slaves. Obsidian chains clinked all around her as many of them were shackled hand and foot. The smell was worse than the latrines near the wheat fields on Delphine's plantation.

The multitude lumbered slowly toward the docks. Ships grew larger as they approached. Aamira paid close attention to the names painted on the sides of the ships but didn't see the *Ephebell.* A sailor shouted in her direction, making her jump in surprise, but the gaunt man was only ordering the captives to move faster so the ships could sail.

The boards of the dock squeaked under the weight of the masses walking toward their fate. Abioye sidled next to Aamira, head bowed, shoulders slumped.

"Are you doing, okay?" he asked.

"I'm fine," she whispered. "These people…I never knew it was this bad. Delphine's plantation was terrible, but our people never suffered like these."

"As bad as it was," Abioye continued, "Delphine certainly isn't the worst. The obsidian chains many slavers use have an effect on reducing the lives and minds of the wearers. They drain everything. It makes them less effective as slaves, but guarantees they'll never rebel." Abioye nodded his head toward a large ship at the end of the large harbor. "That's the *Ephebell*. We need to worry about the second layer of security when it comes to getting off of Vannadale Island."

"I don't understand," Aamira said, suddenly focused on a new worry.

"Abingdale is full of colonial and military checkpoints.

They're going to be inspecting all the older enslaved," Abioye explained. "This rebellion needs to grow. The longer it continues, the faster it will spread across the colonies and into the provinces, igniting the Diaspora to wake up and light the spirit of rebellion. I hope our people fight off and kill all of these witan devils from the western world."

Aamira and Abioye stood in line with their faces covered in moss and dirt, much like the old, broken down, half dead slaves around them. Guards in gray coats and blue capes stood at the gangplank of the ship looking at each slave as they passed, checking their teeth and behind their ears for any signs of infection. Lope Mastiffs barked and growled, sniffing for any contraband. Aamira worried that she still smelled like blood from where the dog had bit her. Even though the wound had magically healed, her clothes still retained the crimson remnants from the puncture.

A man shouted to their left and Aamira recognized the voice. It was General Scipio, Madame Delphine's favorite military partner. He would come to the plantation regularly and dine with the family, Aamira included. He was a handsome witan with blonde hair and beard. Tall and muscular, Scipio always seemed calm, but with a cruelty behind his eyes that always made Aamira keep her distance.

"Sir!" a soldier cried as he pushed his way through the slaves lined up to enter the ship. "General Scipio! One of our men found several of Delphine's slaves trying to get on the Ravenshire sailing to Ruad City. When we beat them, they said there were more runaways here now in the crowds. One of them said Aamira was hiding amongst them."

"Search the crowd, now!" Scipio ordered, pointing at the slaves. "Delphine wants Aamira back. Search all the way back to the village! Find her!"

Panic took hold in Aamira's heart. They were so close, and now everything would fall apart. Solomon had told her that destiny and the gods were calling her to IFF. Braémah made her promise to get there.

"They know I'm here. We need to think of something fast," Aamira whispered to Abioye.

"I'll break cover and draw them away from you," Abioye said.

"No!" Aamira gasped, grabbing Abioye's hand to keep him close.

"Then we do what we can and fight them off," Abioye said.

They couldn't fight off the soldiers. Aamira would be captured and dragged back to the plantation. Abioye would be killed. Reilish, wherever she was in the crowd, would be killed too, as would all the women and children that had trusted her.

But maybe Aamira could do something. She had caused an earthquake less than an hour before, right? It hadn't been on purpose, but she knew it had been her that had done it. Maybe another earthquake would do the trick. But she was over water now on the docks. What could she do? Why hadn't she listened to Solomon? Why hadn't she believed any of this was possible? Why could she not believe in miracles?

Her vision started to blur again like it had in the forest. Her head swam as she reached out mentally for any possibility to help her and the slaves. She felt the water beneath her shifting, splashing against the wooden pillars of the harbor. The air was thick and humid.

They needed to hide. They needed to get on that ship without being seen.

She called on Aarde itself to help her.

And then it happened. A thick fog rose up from the water and swiftly encompassed the entire dock and harbor. People shouted in surprise, crying that they couldn't see anything, and that some witchcraft had enveloped the area.

Even through the thick fog though, Aamira could see clearly. The soldiers stopped in their tracks. The growls of Lope Mastiffs were the only sound beyond the lapping of waves against the pier.

Was it a miracle, or something Aamira should have known how to do before now? She didn't have time to contemplate the answer.

"Aamira, your eyes," Abioye whispered. "They're glowing green."

"I can see through the fog," Aamira replied. "Follow me." Aamira pulled Abioye through the crowd, avoiding the witans, enslavement catchers, and the police. They passed within a few feet of General Scipio, who was screaming at his men about finding their way through the fog. Quickly and without incident, Aamira and Abioye snuck onto the ship and fled to the hold where hundreds of slaves had already been chained. They crouched in a dark corner, unable to avoid the reek all around them.

"I think we're safe for now," Abioye said, wiping the mud from his face as best he could.

"I could use the rest," Aamira said. She could hear shouting through the open cargo doorway across the hold, the fog must have cleared. She watched as Abioye cleaned his face as best he could. She was too tired to even attempt to clear the grime from her skin.

"Hopefully the ship will leave soon," Abioye said as he settled into the corner. A female slave, thin and dirty, breathed rattled breaths beside him.

"Do you think Reilish, and the others are okay?" Aamira asked.

"It doesn't matter," Abioye mumbled.

"What do you mean, 'It doesn't matter?' Of course it matters." Abioye looked at her, anger in his eyes. "Don't you get it? The only reason you and I made it on this ship is because you have abilities, just like Reilish told us. And even with your abilities, you and I are the only ones who will likely make it to IFF. Reilish told me to move forward no matter what and not worry about her or the others. She would do the same in my position. I hope she's safe, but I can only worry about myself now."

Aamira didn't know how to respond to that. Abioye and the others had suffered unspeakable pain and suffering. They had to consider each moment carefully, as it could lead to more pain, or death itself. She had never understood before, but she did now.

Several slaves coughed. The jingling of chains was everpresent.

"I feel bad for all of these enslaved workers who all will die soon," Aamira whispered. Conflicting emotions battled in her heart; compassion for the souls chained around them, and hatred for the people who put them there.

Abioye nodded. "They'll live out the rest of their days with no rest, having to fend for themselves as they're hunted by Dalean soldiers who control and operate these ships. All witans want to see an Aarde with no Black people. This is their way of systematically killing us off and homogenizing the planet in their warped and distorted image."

"Do you hate witans?" Aamira asked as the slave next to her groaned and tried to stretch his legs.

"Yes. Do you?"

That was a hard question for Aamira to answer. She had lived with witans her entire life. Yes, some of them like General Scipio, Madame Delphine, and many of the overseers, were wicked, but others were kind and decent. But even those good people had been taught they were superior to black folk like her. Was it their fault, or the fault of some ancestor who knew better but taught them hate all the same? It was a complicated thing. Words like 'hate' felt too strong, but as she looked around the ship's hold, seeing the suffering men and women, maybe not strong enough at the same time.

Perhaps it was best not to answer.

And so, Aamira sat silently, leaving Abioye's question lingering.

After another hour, sailors closed the cargo door and the ship started moving. Aamira had listened carefully to every word she could hear from the sailors and soldiers. They had searched the crowd but found only a few young slaves sneaking onboard the ships. Several had been whipped right there on the docks. Aamira wondered if Reilish, or any of the runaways from the estate, had been among them.

The dark slave hold had almost no light whatsoever. Occasionally a sailor would open the hatch to the upper deck and a bit of sunlight would peek in, but other than that, there was no way to know what time of day it was or how many hours had passed. At one point, two mariners brought down moldy bread for the slaves and talked about the fighting on the shore. One mentioned they had just passed a small harbor along the Vannadale Pass where the entire village had been burned to the ground. Rebelling slaves had devastated the island.

"It's really happening," Aamira whispered. "The enslaved are rebelling. I guess what Solomon said was true. The signs of the times are upon us."

"The Diaspora have awakened and are doing something about being in forced bondage," Abioye said. "You really met Solomon?"

"I did." Aamira said, thinking of her conversations with her cousins and Solomon in his tent across the street from the coliseum of El Djem.

"The Signs of the Times are upon us," Abioye said under his breath. "How did you meet Solomon? Reilish and the tribe elders would talk about him like he was the servant of the gods themselves. Why did he come to you and not the rest of us?"

"He didn't just come to me," Aamira replied. "My two cousins, Oadira and Heziara, were there too. It all started after the royal rumble about four months ago. I was promised to be one of the breed maids for Nezikiah."

"Nezikiah?" Abioye questioned; eyes wide. "The champion of the fiftieth Royal Rumble?"

"That's the one," Aamira said, rolling her eyes.

"Apologies. I had heard a champion had come to the plantation house to breed with one of the Madame's prize slave stock, but I didn't know it was you, and I didn't know it was Nezikiah. Tales of his victory at the Royal Rumble have been spreading through the slave camps for months."

"Madame Delphine has invested a lot of money in me to bear Nezikiah's children," Aamira said as the ship rocked slightly. "Another generation to participate in the Royal Rumble wrestling tournaments, and Dambé fighting tournaments as well. The Lalaurie family will do whatever it takes to get me back into their possession. Madame Delphine will move mountains and do whatever's necessary to get me back."

"Is that where you met Solomon? At the Rumble?"

"Yes. While at the Coliseum of El Djem, my cousins and I met with Solomon the protector of Aarde and were instructed to leave the colonies as soon as the enslavement rebellions started. He told us that my cousins and I were to do whatever was in our power to get to the outer lands. I was told to get to the Desert Sand

Lands of IFF."

Abioye listened to every word. Aamira could barely make out his face in the dark, but she was glad for his company and interest.

"I recently found out that I'm the Black Madonna of my Bloodline, the Yoruban House," she continued. "Solomon told me the Yorubans have been severed from the holy land of Sahael where the chosen bloodlines once resided before Nata's Invasion."

"What else did Solomon tell you?"

Shame suddenly flowered in Aamira's chest. "Many things," she whispered. "Most of which I didn't pay attention to. I know now that I had become too comfortable in the mansion with my clothes and books. Part of me didn't believe the rebellion on Vannadale would happen, and if not for Braémah, it probably wouldn't have. She listened to Solomon. She believed."

"It's been a hard time for all of us," Abioye agreed. "I didn't believe change could happen either. In fact…" He took a deep breath. "In fact, I was planning on assassinating Madame Lalaurie because I thought nothing would change."

"You were going to kill her?" Aamira asked in shock. "I had been moving between estates," Abioye continued. "I have contacts off the island and have been making my way around for some time trying to help rebels and escapees. I was sent to kill her before the rebellions were to take place. I was also sent to save several of the trafficked girls to gain a better understanding of Madame Delphine's sex trafficking operation, routes and where her headquarters were located in Venn city."

Abioye pulled a piece of cloth from his pocket covered in ink. It looked like a map with directions and information about the inner workings of Abingdale's internal sex-trafficking networks.

"I had no idea this was happening right under my nose," Aamira said.

"It doesn't surprise me. These witan devils will do all that's in their power to wipe out Black females to prevent the reproduction of our kind. It's all because witans are slowly becoming extinct and will dwindle over time. They're doing all they can to prevent their own natural demise. Once I had the freed the woman and gained all the information I needed, that was when the fires started. It was chaos after that. I needed to make it to IFF, which was my plan from the start, but since I didn't think the rebellion would take place, I was caught off-guard just like you. I tried to get Reilish and a few other friends to safety with me, but that obviously didn't go according to plan."

Aamira nodded. Hearing more about Abioye's story made her feel safer somehow. "So, you escaped the slave trade a long time ago?"

"There's more to it than that, but yes."

"Where are you from?"

"I've been all over. I spent a lot of years in Vannadale as a youth. I was captured at one point and beaten as a runaway. Reilish took me in and nursed me back to health. I was forced to work in the orchards. Vannadale was my home for quite a while." He smiled as he recounted, as if memories flickered before his eyes. "Reilish is wonderful. She was like a mother to so many of the youth in the slave camps. I hope she's alright."

"You've been other places though too?" Aamira asked. She had traveled more than most slaves, since she almost always accompanied Madame Delphine on her journeys, but the desire to pick her own destination had often excited her imagination.

"I've tried to be an agent for change," Abioye nodded. "But it has been far harder than I thought it would be. Our people are beaten down. Many of them are too tired to fight back. The fact that the rebellion took place at all, and has been so successful, raises my hopes for the remnants of Alkebulan and the holy city of Sahael."

"The women that were with you who couldn't speak," Aamira said. "Were they the ones you had rescued?"

"Yes, and if I hadn't seen the Marula Tree and the emerald light emanating from your lookout hole, I believe we would've been caught. I hope they made it onto the ship, or at least one of the ships leaving Vannadale. I wanted so badly to help them, and now it might have been for nothing."

"It wasn't for nothing," Aamira assured. "I wouldn't have made it without you. Hopefully everyone escaped and makes it to their destination as planned. Can I travel with you once we reach IFF in the north? I don't know where I'm going."

Abioye shook his head. "No, all you told me was that you needed to get to the Desert Sand Lands of IFF. That is where our agreement ends."

"So, you'll leave me and these old people to be hunted down like animals by Dalean forces?" Aamira asked, suddenly less comfortable than she had been a moment before.

"You aren't my responsibility, and neither are these people." Abioye said. "I can't think about any one person. This experience has proven that to me. My plans need to be bigger."

Aamira was beside herself but refused to accept Abioye's ultimatum. He was a good man. She knew it. He wouldn't abandon her or anyone else, no matter what he said.

"No. I'm coming with you whether you like it or not. I don't know if that's clear enough for you to understand," Aamira demanded.

"It's loud and clear, and you can think it all you want, but the bottom line is still the bottom line," Abioye said, scooting away from Aamira as far as he could in the tight quarters. "You're not coming with me and that's final. You think you get to direct people however you want to because you think you're special. Did it ever occur to you that it's because of you that Reilish and the others aren't here with us right now? They could be dead, all because Delphine was hunting you."

"I helped hide all of you in the forest," Aamira protested, voice growing louder. "I frightened away the slave hunters by making the ground shake. Don't put all of this on me."

Abioye leaned back against the wooden wall and closed his eyes. "I recommend you get some sleep. When we approach the next checkpoint at the mouth of Vannadale Pass, we'll need to be wary. Once we sail north through it, we'll go our separate ways."

"You're really serious, aren't you?" Aamira asked as sadness and frustration pulled on the muscles of her neck.

"I'm dead serious," Abioye said candidly. He turned his back to Aamira to get some rest.

"Fine!" Aamira said as she folded her arms.

"Rest well," Abioye said.

Aamira couldn't tell what time of day it was or how long she had slept. The hold was perpetually dark. Luckily, she had grown used to the smell, but as far as she knew, days had passed as easily as hours.

She longed to see the sun and breathe fresh air, but if the sailors saw her too closely, they would assume she had escaped during the rebellion since she was young and healthy, unlike the other slaves around her. The safest thing would be to stay hidden as long as possible.

Abioye had moved sometime during the night and no longer rested beside her. His abandonment stung worse than Aamira thought it would. What would she do when they reached IFF? Where would she go? Solomon hadn't given her many instructions beyond getting to the continent. That was one thing she remembered, his vagueness. Another reason she had stopped listening during his lessons.

In the darkness though, the other slaves felt free to talk. Whispers moved from one side of the hold to the other. Word had spread that Aamira was among them. She learned that not only did they want to protect her if they could, but that several of the escaped slaves from the estate had in fact made it onto the ship. Aamira didn't know where they were, or even who they were, but the fact even a handful had made it, brightened her spirits.

After a few hours, the cry came from above deck that land was in their sights.

"From what I'm hearing," an old man with scarred hands and gray hair whispered to Aamira as he passed messages throughout the ship, "there's nowhere to dock the vessels. I'm also getting word that a group of colonial soldiers have set up additional check points. They're inspecting every Dalen ship with enslaved people before they make their departure to the Desert Sand Lands of IFF, and before we all become live hunting bait."

"Will they enter the ships to search?" Aamira asked.

The old man shrugged. "I don't know. You can feel the vessel slowing though. We'll dock within minutes. Then they'll ring the bell for us to exit the hold. I've done this many times before."

"We need to be ready," a firm voice answered. Through the darkness, Aamira saw Abioye moving toward her through the slaves. "They don't really enter the ships, but if we're forced to disembark, we're in trouble," Abioye continued. He crouched down and handed Aamira some bread. Unlike the moist and moldy rations, she had enjoyed since getting on the ship, this was fresh and delicious.

"Where did you get this?" she asked.

"I stole a bit from the middeck while the guards were talking," Abioye replied. "It's not much, but it will do. This witan bitch just won't give up, will she? Madame Delphine will do anything to show that we're all inferior compared to her fake sense of witan supremacy."

"What do you mean?" she asked.

Abioye took a bite of bread. "I heard the sailors talking about the checkpoints. They're being run by Delphine's people. General Scipio sent men to the mouth of Vannadale Pass on horseback. She really wants to find you, doesn't she?"

I'm worth a lot I suppose," Aamira said as she swallowed the last bite of her bread. "It's more than that, though. Delphine doesn't like to lose. Her entire life has been a competition with her sisters. I've seen it many times as they talk at the Royal Rumble each time we went. Being in that family would be like hell on Aarde. She can't stomach losing. And maybe…"

Aamira paused. Part of her hoped that somewhere deep down, Delphine cared for Aamira; that there was more to her hunt than just money.

"And maybe what?" Abioye asked.

"Maybe she wants me back because…she cares for me." A breath blew from Abioye's nose. It wasn't angry or dismissive.

"You lived with her most of your life," Abioye said, tapping Aamira's knee. "As depressing as it sounds, she's probably like family to you."

Neck muscles tightening, Aamira tried hard to keep her emotions in-check. “Yes,” she whispered.

Abioye put his arm around her as she cried silently. He held her close. His skin was warm.

“This whole thing has been a bit more complicated for you, hasn’t it?” Abioye asked. “I didn’t realize it before. I’m sorry. For the rest of us, the rebellion was about anger and hate, and all of that. For you, there was love there too. I thought you were having a hard time because you missed the comforts of the manor and the easy life, but I get it now. The people in that house were the only family you ever knew.”

Sobs echoed quietly through the corner of the hold. Abioye’s words pierced Aamira like a lance. She hadn’t realized it herself, but much of her hesitancy, her reluctance to listen to Solomon or prepare for the rebellion, was because even as bad as things had been in that house, it was the only home she had ever known. Delphine, Braémah, the servant girls, even the gardeners who trimmed the bushes around the manor and would make crude comments about Aamira’s breasts, had been a twisted family unit. Every one of them had been a slave in their own way. Aamira was now free of them, but her heart ached all the same. It was a tragic truth that she couldn’t escape.

Abioye comforted Aamira, helping her gain control of her emotions once more.

“Let’s figure out something together,” he soothed, “We both are going to have to find a way to get past Madame Delphine’s additional checkpoints and surprise inspections. Doing it together will be easier than by ourselves.”

“Thank you,” Aamira said, slowly wiping away her emerald tears.

“Your eyes are bright green now, so there is no way you’ll make it past inspection without someone noticing you,” Abioye warned.

“We need to figure something out fast,” Aamira said.

“Indeed, we do,” Abioye said.

Aamira’s stomach started to knot up, as perspiration formed around her forehead. A bell rang for the slaves to depart the ships just as the old man had warned.

The slaves stood slowly and moved toward the closed ramp door. Light poured into the hold as the door lowered. Aamira closed her eyes against the bright glare. She hadn’t seen sunlight in at least two days. Abioye held her close as the mass of people lumbered toward the ramp. They stepped over several dead bodies as they made their way toward the exit. A number of slaves hadn’t even made it this far before perishing into the darkness. The ship was docked at a small fishing port with huts on the shore and a weathered wooden building where men were slicing open large carp and other fish. The strong smell didn’t bother Aamira after the stench of the ship itself. The breeze felt good on her face. Soldiers in blue capes stood on the docks in orderly rows checking each slave individually before sending them back to the ship in another que.

“Just move with the line for now,” Abioye said as they stepped into the sunlight of morning. “We have some time before we’ll be inspected. Can you do the thing with the fog again? Maybe an earthquake?”

“I think so, but they’ll just check the ship again once the fog lifts or the ground stops shaking.”

“What other powers do you have?”

Aamira’s bracelet started to glow as she thought about all the things Solomon had tried to teach her. Conjuring blades was a good one, and she was better at it after having practiced, but she couldn't fight off all the soldiers no matter how much magic she had.

What else could she do? Solomon had told her she could communicate with animals, and Aamira had once seen through the eyes of a mouse during their training, but that wouldn't help them now either.

*What else? What else? What else?* She whispered to herself.

Skin-change.

The ability to take on the appearance of someone else.

Solomon said it was more advanced but could be done for short periods during times of duress.

Now was definitely a time of duress.

Aamira looked around at the old men and women around her as they slowly moved toward the checkpoint. How would she change her appearance when she didn't know how to do it. Nervous sweat dripped from her nose. She closed her eyes and tried to feel as she had when touching the ground and sending out the earthquake.

*Change your shape. Change your shape.*

Her bracelet glowed bright again, and as if in response, a sharp pain shot from her forehead down to her toes. She cried out and fell into Abioye.

"Are you okay?" he asked, looking around the crowd.

"It…hurts," Aamira said between grit teeth.

The pain burned more intensely, and Aamira thought she would die.

"Oi!" a soldier shouted. "What's all the yelling about over here?"

"Nothing sir," Abioye replied, still holding Aamira close.

"You're a bit young for being on this ship, boy," another soldier said. "What are you doing here?"

The pain began to subside, and Aamira opened her eyes to see three soldiers standing in front of them wearing the blue capes of General Scipio's army.

"He asked you a question, boy," the third soldier said, hand grabbing his sword hilt. "Who's the old lady with you?"

Abioye looked down at Aamira and she saw his eyes widen.

"She's…" Abioye stuttered. "My mother," he said quickly.

What was Abioye talking about? Who was his mother? Then Aamira looked down at her hand and saw the wrinkles and dark spots on the skin.

She had skin-changed! She looked like an old woman, just as she had wanted.

"Your mother, eh?" the first soldier said, grabbing Aamira's face.

"I…got permission to come with her and keep her safe," Abioye replied quickly. "The men from the manor told me I'd be hunted with the rest of them once we arrived on IFF, but I can't leave my mother. I don't care what happens to me."

One of the bloodhounds rushed over and barked at Aamira. The lead soldier kicked the animal.

"Get back mutt! You're supposed to sniff out the girl, not old ladies, and their stupid sons. Get back!"

The soldiers sent Aamira and Abioye on their way with the other slaves. Within a half hour, they were back in their same hiding spots and relaxed once more. As soon as the door to the hold closed, intense pain once again racked Aamira's body as she returned to her normal appearance. Afterward, she slumped back against the wood hull covered in sweat and completely exhausted.

"How did you do that?" Abioye asked.

"Solomon…told me…I could," she breathed. "I focused on how…I felt when I…sent out that tremor in the…woods. I worked."

"Yeah, it did," Abioye smiled.

"That was some…fast thinking back there when you told them…I was your mother."

"I didn't know what else to say. I'm just glad that dog came up barking and they sent us away quick. You don't have the brand of MDL on your right shoulder like the other slaves. If they had inspected you closer, they may have noticed that, and it could have caused us problems."

The ship lurched as it rocked in the water and reentered the passage. Aamira rested for most of the day. Abioye stayed by her side, making sure rations made their way to her and that any sailors who entered the hold didn't notice her.

"Thank you for staying with me," Aamira said. "I thought you were going to abandon me."

"I thought I was going to as well," Abioye replied. "But I guess you're harder to abandon than I thought. Plus, anyone who can cause earthquakes and change their shape is someone worth keeping by your side, I guess. We will arrive in the Desert Sand Lands in a fortnight."

"So, I can come with you?" Aamira asked.

"Yes," Abioye said.

Aamira smiled. Maybe she wouldn't be alone on the journey after all. Maybe she would make it to IFF and find out why Solomon wanted her to go there in the first place. Maybe she could help her people along the way.

Maybe.

# CHAPTER III

# STOWAWAYS

Vannadale Pass, Straits, Desert Sand Lands of IFF

Fourteen days had passed. The only reason Aamira was aware of that fact was because a cry had just gone out that another ship was detaining the *Ephebell* for search before it could dock in the closest IFF port. Those two weeks had been the worst of Aamira's life. Darkness and death permeated the air itself. The food had been worse than meager. If not for Abioye's ability to steal rations, Aamira knew she would have lost far more weight. At least 30 slaves had died during the short voyage, their bodies taken by sailors and tossed unceremoniously overboard. Aamira had gotten to know many of the slaves and listened to their stories intently. Their lives had been full of torment and pain, yes, but also love and personal sacrifice. The women spoke of their children and grandchildren while the men regaled her of tales of how they swept their wives off their feet while working in the fields and protected them against being raped by slavers, often being whipped for their efforts. They smiled and said they would do it again gladly.

After fourteen days, Aamira had grown to love these people like she had never loved anyone in her life, outside her cousins

Oadira and Heziara. She felt shame that she hadn't been more active in the rebellion but made a commitment to herself that she would never turn her back on her people again.

"The crewmen are coming to inspect the ship," Abioye said as he ran down the steps from middeck. "They are scanning all the old women and men, with instructions to look for all of their branding marks."

"We should be close to the Desert Sand Lands of IFF," Aamira said, standing up.

"We are several hours away still," Abioye replied. "We need to hurry and find someplace else to hide," Aamira said.

Abioye grabbed Aamira by the arm. "We need to act fast. I know this ship well. It's the ship that I took when I smuggled into Vannadale. I know where all of the hiding places are that will allow us access to the top deck of the ship. That's how I've been able to smuggle food and bring it here down so easily."

"Okay, I'll follow your lead," Aamira said.

Aamira and Abioye stealthily climbed the stairs to the second level of the ship. The area was deserted. Two chairs sat before a long hallway with numerous doors on either side. Lanterns hung on the walls providing light.

"Normally there are guards here," Abioye said as they stepped past the chairs. He pulled one of the lanterns from the wall to light their path. "This is where they keep obsidian nitrate bombs."

"They have bombs on the ship?" Aamira gasped. "Why?" "They're shipping them to IFF for the Dales." Abioye grabbed her arm again and pulled her down the hallway. He opened one of the doors on their right and shone the lantern inside. Dozens of iron-wrought bombs three feet tall filled the space along with a series of tall wooden crates. "I have an idea," Abioye continued. "We can make a trail that leads back to this pile. I can create a spark that would blow out the ship's back side, allowing us the ability to escape."

Aamira stared at the bombs. She shook her head. "No. The Ship is still hours away from anchoring in IFF. The ship would sink if we blew part of it up. Everyone would have to fend for themselves getting to the sand shores. None of them would make it. Not one."

"I told you," Abioye continued. "We can't save these people. They're going to die as wargame prey anyway." "So, that makes it okay for you and me to kill them now?" Abioye's head dropped.

"We need to find another way," Aamira urged. "My life isn't worth more than theirs because I'm young or because Solomon told me I had a destiny. I won't put myself above anyone else ever again. We better think of something."

"Let's get to the top deck of the ship," Abioye breathed. "We'll have a better view from up there, and maybe we can find an alternative."

As they closed the door on the bomb storage area, Abioye opened another room full of cloth and laundry for the crew quarters.

"Put this on," he said, handing Aamira a dirty sheet that smelled of body odor. "Wrap yourself in it. The slave women on the upper decks cover themselves against the heat of the day. We'll blend in."

They climbed up to the deck quietly. The sun was drifting toward the west in its late afternoon journey. In the distance, Aamira saw pale yellow sand dunes under a blue sky. Hot, dry air chapped her lips almost immediately.

She and Abioye ducked behind one of the masts but were spotted by a group of enslaved women in chains who were cleaning the ship's deck with mops and brushes. Aamira placed her finger over her mouth, asking the women for silence. They nodded and went back to their cleaning.

Aamira's bracelet started emanating and pulsating once more. It seemed the piece of jewelry either knew things she didn't about dangers around her, or it felt her mood and responded to her anxiety. Either way, now was a time of action.

A second ship had pulled beside the *Ephebell* and linked the two vessels with ropes and hooks. A group of six soldiers spoke to the *Ephebell* captain and his sailors, Three of the soldiers had already started inspecting the slave women while they cleaned.

"Check their brands," The lead soldier said as he wiped sweat from his forehead with a handkerchief. "Anyone without a brand is a stowaway from the Vannadale rebellions. The Dales only purchased old slaves with the brand. Check them all and bring any non-branded slaves to me."

"Yes sir!" the other soldiers shouted.

Abioye looked around. "We have to blow the ship now," he hissed.

What could they do? Aamira knew of at least 20 escaped slaves onboard. Plus, she wouldn't leave the branded slaves to be used as target practice by the Dales.

Her bracelet glowed again.

Yes. Now was a time for action.

"Go," she whispered to Abioye.

"Go where?"

"Go and spread the alarm to the slaves that the back half of the ship is about to explode. I'll do what I can up here."

"What are you talking about?" Abioye asked. Confusion deepened the lines on his face.

Aamira formed an emerald blade in her right hand. The energy crackled, but the weapon remained solid in her grasp. She focused on the captain as he stood with his back to her hiding place, a set of keys hanging from his belt.

"You'll need keys to unlock the slaves," Aamira said, eyes focused on that belt. "Give me a minute."

She slowly stood up, letting the sheet fall from her head and shoulders.

"What are you doing?" Abioye whispered frantically.

*That's a good question,* Aamira thought. *I'm doing something. I'm finally doing something.*

She smiled as she took a step forward. It may be a reckless something. It may be a stupid something.

But it was something.

Before she could talk herself out of it, Aamira leaped forward. The stories of the enslaved men and women, the lives that had been taken from them, the pain they had endured, erupted inside her like a volcano. A second sword manifested in her left hand. She charged the captain and with a single swipe, severed the man's head. The other guards and soldiers stumbled back in shock, allowing Aamira to respond. She swung each sword, clumsily, but quickly. Two more soldiers fell, along with three soldiers.

"The princess fights for us!" a slave woman cried. She took her mop and smashed it against the head of the closest soldier.

The top deck exploded into pandemonium.

Aamira reached down and yanked the keys from the dead captain's belt.

“Here!” she called, tossing the keys to Abioye. “Set them all free, and then do what you have to!”

Abioye stood there for a second, holding the keys in his hand. As if regaining consciousness, he darted to the stairs, punching a sailor in the face as he went.

Two more sailors fell beneath Aamira’s blades. She felt powerful and strong, as if nothing could stop her. Why had she been hesitant to learn her artes from Solomon? What witan fear had taken hold in her heart and mind? Now she let it all go as she hacked and sliced her way across the bridge.

Slaves began running up the stairs and joining the fight. Even though they were old and weak, a madness seemed to consume them as they swarmed their captors.

“Fight back!” Aamira screamed. “Fight back and---”

Pain emanated from her leg as a sword sliced her thigh. A soldier rushed her, blood on his blade.

“Die, bitch!” he cried.

Aamira stumbled back, feeling blood drip down her wounded leg. The soldier advanced, swiping the air between them. Aamira tried to block his blow, but his speed and skill easily outmatched her.

Just as he pulled back to stab her in the chest, a rope looped over his head and yanked back at his neck. Abioye wrapped the rope tightly against the man’s throat and squeezed mercilessly. The sword fell from the soldier’s hand as he tried to grab Abioye’s head.

“Now you die!” Abioye seethed through grit teeth.

Eyes wide, hands grasping, the soldier gasped his last and fell against the wooden deck lifeless.

“Are you okay?” Abioye asked, rushing to Aamira’s side.

"It hurts," she replied.

"More soldiers are coming over from the other ship!"

Amira glanced over as several slaves were cut down by guards and sailors. "What about---"

A large explosion ripped through the ship and cut off Aamira's question. Heat consumed the air and the vessel rocked back and forth. The back of the ship lurched upward. Debris flew all around.

Abioye grabbed Aamira and pulled her toward the side. "Everyone has been released. They know they need to swim, and I told them to hold onto the chunks of wood in the water, It will help them stay afloat."

"Everyone swim to the sand shores!" Aamira ordered. She and Abioye leaped from the side as more soldiers rushed the *Ephebell* top deck. At least two hundred other slaves joined them in the cool water, grabbing whatever debris they could to keep from drowning. Sailors who hadn't been killed in the blast jumped to the ocean as well, but were met by angry slaves who swarmed them, pushing them beneath the surface until they drowned.

"Swim!" Aamira cried. "Swim toward the shore! Hold to pieces of the ship to stay afloat if you need to."

The currents pushed toward the sandy horizon. Every so often Aamira looked back at the *Ephebell*. It sank quickly, as did the adjacent vessel, which had been damaged in the blast as well. The soldiers, laden in their heavy armor, perished quickly once they abandoned ship.

Not a single soldier or sailor made it to shore. Miraculously, almost every slave managed to hold on and crawl onto the beach. When Aamira felt sand between her toes, she started to cry, falling to her knees, and thanking Ishtar and Obatala for such an amazing blessing. The gash on her leg stung in the salt water, but it was a small discomfort in comparison to her joy.

Her moment of peace was short lived.

"We need to hurry," Abioye said as he helped an old woman out of the water. "The other ships will start hunting us. We're not far from the port. Reports are probably already going out of the *Ephebell* sinking and our escape."

"Witans are awful," Aamira said.

Abioye nodded. "Indeed, they are also here to catch any healthy slaves and bring them back to Vannadale."

"Where are we going?" a hunched man asked as he squeezed sea water from his gray dreadlocks. "Most of us can't travel far without a rest."

"There's a tent camp a few hours walk from here," Abioye said, pointing over the dunes to the northeast. "If we follow the coast and then turn to the north, we'll reach it before dark, but we have to hurry."

Aamira stepped forward, looking at all the escaped slaves, most old and weak, as the waves crashed behind them.

"I know you're tired," she shouted. "But we need to travel if we want to remain free. Everyone who escaped from Vannadale who are still strong, help the aged as best you can. We have a couple hours of travel still ahead of us."

The conclave started walking through the sand, making their way slowly along the coast. Abioye led the way, with Aamira by his side. The air was hot and dry. Aamira longed for a drink of water and could only imagine how the old men and women were suffering. Even as the sun moved closer to the horizon and the sky grew pink in the west, the heat never abated.

"Too many of these people are going to die before we reach the tent camp," Abioye said after a half hour of walking. "It's a miracle so many of them made it to shore. How's your leg?"

"It's doing pretty well," Aamira answered, rubbing the cut on her thigh. It didn't seem as deep as it was back on the ship. She looked over her shoulder at the mass of people behind her. "I can't imagine what it would be like to be trafficked as young girls and then used as bait to capture more black women for the Abingdale province."

"Did Madame Delphine really do that?" Abioye asked. "She would use young girls to trap older women who came to help them?"

"Yes. She would take me to the docks with her sometimes and I would see all of the young Black women and little girls. They would come in from the Desert Lands of IFF to be prepped, blooded, and sold to the Lalaurie Estates in the Lucedale, Vannadale, and Abingdale provinces. She and the captains would talk about placing the girls on the roads until a family would find them and take them back to their homes to help them. Slavers would then capture the entire family and enslave them. The women were sought after most of all."

"For the purpose of pleasing witan men and women," Abioye said, wiping sweat from his forehead.

"Indeed, but there are other uses also," Aamira said.

"For replenishing the provinces." Abioye spat as if disgusted by the thought. "More slaves to breed a bigger workforce, and then place them on various sex farms. It's why I was sent to chop the head off the snake,"

"Who sent you to kill her?" Aamira asked. "You said you spent a lot of time in Vannadale as a youth, but that means you've been to many other places."

"It was my mission to find a way to infiltrate Madame Delphine's sex trafficking operation. Reilish  was my contact on the inside, but it became too difficult for her to share information without exposing her and risking the lives of others on the Estate."

Aamira nodded. “That is dangerous. If they were caught it could’ve cost the lives of her entire family, and even those who were close to her.”

Sand shifted under their feet as they walked. Abioye remained quiet for a moment.

“She understood the risks,” he said eventually. “And the rewards. Reilish knew her efforts would bring Delphine’s whole operation down, crippling the Abingdale colonies. The rebellions were the first phase in bringing down the large enterprises of the Lalaurie’s in the colonies.”

After another half hour of walking, Abioye turned the group north from the sand coast into a forest of juniper trees and cactus. The sand gave way to rocks and cliffs. They rested for a few minutes before Abioye urged the group onward. The sun was setting and the temperatures growing more pleasant.

“At least it’s not so hot now,” Aamira said as they walked through the juniper trees.

“It won’t last,” Abioye warned. “Once the sun sets, it gets cold pretty fast out here. We need to reach the tent camp soon.”

“Once we arrive, where do we go from there?” Aamira asked.

“We’ll figure that out once we’re there,” Abioye replied. “I’m more worried about soldiers from the port tracking us down.”

“Something has to be done to stop the slave trade, and trafficking,” Aamira said, feeling the sweat chill on her skin. “Surely you and I can figure out a way to end this terrible practice.”

Abioye shook his head. “I’m not sure. I don’t think that there is anything you or I can do right now. We should focus on getting to safety. As soon as those ships get to these shores, they will do all that it is in their power to track all of us down.”

Darkness spread, but as they reached a rocky ridge, Aamira smelled campfire on the air. Below in a small sand valley, the lights of fires could be seen. Abioye led them to the small camp where they were welcomed by travelers who guarded the waypoint. A well of water acted as the centerpiece of the camp, and everyone took turns drinking and replenishing their spirits.

Aamira peered through the dark, seeing what looked like Marula trees surrounding the camp. They grew from the sand, something she had never seen before.

"There's not enough food for everyone," Abioye told Aamira after he had spoken with the chieftain of the camp. "But they'll share what they have. Chief Gavrel and his clan are used to having groups stop here, so they have enough bedrolls to keep everyone from getting too cold. Drink and sleep. Everyone here will have my protection and the protection of my family."

"Who is your family?" Aamira asked. Abioye hadn't mentioned a family before. She had assumed Reilish was as close to any family he had.

"My father's people will be here soon. We need to continue traveling inland to meet them," Abioye said.

"Who is your family?" Aamira repeated. "Who's your father?"

"Get some rest," Abioye said, face emotionless. He placed his hand on Aamira's shoulder and walked off.

After procuring her bedroll, Aamira lay down under the stars thinking about the escape from the ship, Abioye's strange evasion, and the fact that she had killed several men that day.

She had killed people.

No regret or shame touched her mind at the thought. Instead, a deep thrill tingled her skin as she remembered stomping toward the men and killing each of them with a single stroke from her blades. She was powerful, just as Solomon had told her. She could defend herself and the people around her. No slaver would survive a confrontation with her ever again. Witans would come to fear the sound of her name.

Aamira would spill more blood, and she would revel in it.

The group left the camp first thing in the morning, continuing north. They walked through the Marula trees Aamira had noticed the night before. As she had guessed, they grew directly from the sand with no grass or other plants at their base, as if they were the only plants that could flourish in this harsh environment.

"This island is different than I expected," Aamira said as she walked up to Abioye. His talk of family the night before intrigued her, and she wanted to see if she could glean more details from him. She would start the conversation innocently enough before delving deeper. "There are Marula Trees everywhere around here," she continued, "but the land is all sand. I've never seen anything like it before or heard of anything like this."

"Chieftain Gavrel told me a slave camp moved through this area recently," Abioye said, completely bypassing Aamira's comment. "We still have time and considerable distance between us and them, but we need to be wary."

"Sooner or later, we're going to have to fight them," Aamira said.

"Most likely," Abioye replied as he looked up at the Marula branches overhead. "You did well yesterday. You caught me off-guard when you attacked the captain, but you did well."

"It felt good," Aamira smiled.

After two hours of walking, they exited the trees and reentered the open dunes. The sun now baked down on them mercilessly. Abioye kept them moving at a steady pace.

They soon arrived at an abandoned slave-catching encampment with dead witan and black bodies everywhere. Obsidian cages sat in the sun with women and girls left inside to die. The three cages could house up to 25 prisoners at once.

"Some of them are still alive!" Aamira shouted as she pulled on the locks. A teenage girl opened her eyes and looked weakly up at Aamira. "We need to get them open!"

"We need help!" Abioye called to the people behind them. Aamira manifested a green ax and began hacking at the lock. After a few strokes, the cage door swung open and she pulled out the young woman, along with seven other girls who were still alive. Aamira then ran to the other cages and did the same.

"It's okay we're here to help and free you all. You're all safe around us," Aamira said.

"Someone's approaching," Abioye said, pointing toward a dune to their left. The newly freed girls began whimpering and ran back into their cages.

"Why are they running to the cages?" Aamira asked.

"They're afraid," Abioye answered.

"Of who?"

A man stepped to the top of the dune, sun shining against his billowing black cape. He stood six feet eight inches tall, possessing dark chocolate skin and a chiseled muscular physique. A hood covered his head, while a mask obscured his features from the nose down. Only his piercing eyes could be seen.

No one moved.

"A Hashashin," Abioye whispered with a hint of awe.

"Who?" Aamira asked.

"An assassin," Abioye said, glancing around at all the witan bodies lying in the sand. Abioye smiled. "They kill their enemies with deadly precision. The Hashashin dot the IFF forest and the dunes, keeping local travelers safe. Their purpose is to kill men who put their hands on Alkebulan women unworthily. Women can summon the Hashashin through the female prayer of deliverance."

The Hashashin assassin stepped slowly down the sand, leaving footprints behind him. He held his hands away from his body to show he carried no weapon as he approached Aamira. He bowed his head.

"You will always be protected and watched over as the sacred blood," The Hashashin Assassin said.

"How do you know I'm of the sacred blood?" Aamira questioned.

The Hashashin nodded his head as if motioning toward her face.

"Your eyes say everything I need to know," he looked over at Abioye. "As does the man you travel with." The assassin removed his hood and mask, smiling bright white teeth. Small braids hung from his head and a trim beard covered his chin. "It is good to see you again, Abioye."

"I knew it was you!" Abioye grinned. He stepped forward and embraced the man.

"Wait what? Y'all know each other?" Aamira asked. Who was Abioye? She thought she had him figured out, but ever since they arrived in the sand lands, he seemed to be a completely different person.

"This is Adewara, my father's most trusted advisor," Abioye chuckled. "I wasn't sure what happened here, but when I saw a Hashashin on the dune, it all made sense."

"I have been looking for you for some time," Adewara said. He glanced at Aamira for a moment and then returned his gaze to Abioye. "I was trying to free the women from the cages when I heard you approaching. I thought you might be Dales from the coast, so I hid along the ridgeline until I realized who you were."

Abioye shook his head and hugged the man again. "How have you been?"

"I've been fine! It has been nearly three weeks since I received your last message. Were you successful in your mission?"

"I...was not," Abioye said, dropping his head slightly.

Adewara looked at Aamira. "It matters not. As Solomon promised so many years ago, a Princess of Sahael is in our midst. This is a triumph that cannot be overstated. You did well, my prince."

"Prince?" Aamira asked. He was a prince now? What happened to the young man who had been captured as a youth and spent years among the slaves of Lalaurie's plantation learning from Reilish?

"We can discuss that later," Abioye said. He turned to look at Adewara. "And honestly, it wasn't on purpose that I brought her here. Up until the voyage, I planned on making the journey alone."

"Did you not recognize her green eyes, and the signs of the times?" Adewara asked, face growing serious.

Again, Abioye dropped his gaze. "You know my thoughts on that subject."

Adewara put his hand on Abioye's shoulder. "And hopefully the circumstances that brought you here with a member of the royal bloodline, along with all these freed slaves, will give you a little faith for once. This has been the will of Ishtar and Obatala, whether you choose to believe it or not."

Faith. Aamira couldn't judge Abioye's lack of belief. She had never been one to show faith in what she couldn't see. During the planning of the rebellion, as Solomon and Braémah tried to explain to her how things would work and why people would fight back, she hadn't believed it would happen. She hadn't believed in her own power either. But here she was, standing on the dunes of the Sand Lands of IFF just as Solomon promised her she would, hearing that he had told the people here the same thing.

Maybe belief was more powerful than she had given credit.

"How have you come to be here?" Abioye asked.

"Witan enslavers caught many young, innocent girls that were going to be sent to Abingdale to be trafficked," Adewara replied. "I had to intervene to save them; by doing so, I learned that they had been trapped and tricked by their own people. They were quickly disposed of by my assassins. I was able to glean all the information needed out of them. I learned that General Scipio has started his operation of invading and occupying the desert lands of IFF. And I received word this morning he is hunting specifically for a member for the royal bloodline." He looked Aamira in the eye. "You may have lived in secret on the plantation, but now your identity has been laid bare. Delphine apparently knows who you are now."

"An entire military operation just for me?" Aamira asked.

"Operation Red Dog is a Naval campaign created to systematically wipe out every black male, and to traffic every single black girl and woman of Yoruban descent," Adewara explained. "But you are worth far more than any concubine or virgin bride ever could be. You are one of the princesses of Sahael, which means Natas himself will be coming for you. For that reason alone, Delphine would move heaven and Aarde itself. To present one of the princesses to Natas, one of the girls he has hunted since the overthrow of Sahael, would grant an individual power and prestige beyond any king or queen. Scipio will stop at nothing to get you back now. Dark clouds gather, and war threatens our land like never before."

Aamira looked around at all the women and little girls. "What will happen to the people in IFF? What about the slaves here?"

"They would have been killed for sport and then fed to the alligators and sharks," Adewara said. "But you have stopped that from happening. Still, General Scipio will go to every city and round up every Yoruban male to kill them. They will kill all of the males, and torture the female through trafficking, systematically wiping them out."

"We need to make our way to these cities and gather up these scattered Yorubans that are hiding amongst the people on this island," Aamira said, with conviction in her voice.

Abioye stepped between Aamira and Adewara. "Now isn't the time. There are matters that are more pressing."

"What's more pressing than a war that could wipe all of us out?" Aamira asked, pulse quickening. "A war being brought here because of me? What's more pressing than that?"

"Yes, the prince is right. We need to get going," Adewara said. "The Signs of the Times are upon us. The Hashashin assassins will guide us back through the forest to the city of Bethdin. I will send out the call that will bring them back to us within the hour. From there, we will see what will become of this land and this people.

Adewara pulled a horn from his belt and blew a crisp loud note.

"My Hashashin brothers will be here soon. Let us make our way back to the south toward the forest in the meantime. Follow me."

Sweat dripped from Aamira's brow as they set off behind Adewara. Abioye remained silent and stoic. The slaves, still weak and tired, trotted along slowly, but with courage.

War was coming. A war that was focused on a single person.

Aamira had been a woman of fear and inaction for most of her life. But that was all over now. She had fought. She had killed. She wanted to kill again.

Let the war come.

Aamira wasn't afraid anymore.

**[To be continued on Volume 2 Book 2]**

OUT NOW:

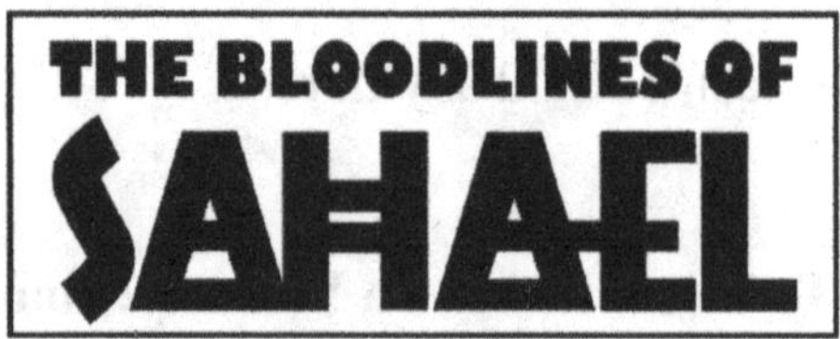


VOLUME TWO

BOOK TWO

*THE THIRD SIGN*

www.ingramcontent.com/pod-product-compliance
Lightning Source LLC
Chambersburg PA
CBHW010448310726
48979CB00018B/2852/J

* 9 7 8 1 9 6 3 0 8 9 2 7 1 *